EXTRA INNINGS

EXTRA INNINGS

THE DIAMOND THIEVES

B.W. GIBSON

authorHOUSE®

AuthorHouse™ LLC
1663 Liberty Drive
Bloomington, IN 47403
www.authorhouse.com
Phone: 1-800-839-8640

Published by AuthorHouse 05/19/2014

ISBN: 978-1-4918-5663-5 (sc)
ISBN: 978-1-4918-5662-8 (hc)
ISBN: 978-1-4918-5661-1 (e)

Library of Congress Control Number: 2014901678

Any people depicted in stock imagery provided by Thinkstock are models,
and such images are being used for illustrative purposes only.
Certain stock imagery © Thinkstock.

This book is printed on acid-free paper.

Because of the dynamic nature of the Internet, any web addresses or links contained in
this book may have changed since publication and may no longer be valid. The views
expressed in this work are solely those of the author and do not necessarily reflect the
views of the publisher, and the publisher hereby disclaims any responsibility for them.

Written by B.W. Gibson

Edited by Mary Kay Landon

Cover Art by Adam Lichi

www.bwgibson.net

A Special Thank You to Wes and Marilyn Gibson, Aaron Smith, Kyle Brown and all my family and friends that supported and helped me throughout this endeavor.

1

Today was their thirteenth birthday.

It was Saturday, June 21, 1947 and summer was off to a great start. Identical twins Jimmy and Billy McGee were upstairs in their spacious, attic bedroom of their parents' three-story home in Eugene, Mississippi. Both boys would have preferred to be outdoors playing baseball with their friends but the McGee family house rule was that birthdays were to be spent at home with the family. This year, however, Billy designed a plan that would allow them to see their friends. In order for it to work he and Jimmy needed to be upstairs in their bedroom. They would have to make enough noise to wake their toddler brother, whose bedroom was downstairs, directly across the hall from the attic door. If this happened, their mother would want them as far away from the house as possible.

Billy stared up from his bed at his five model fighter planes suspended at different lengths from the vaulted ceiling. He then looked over at the clock on his nightstand. It was almost noon. Their friend Skip would soon be showing up to perform his role in Billy's plan. Jimmy was relaxing in his bed reading one of his Detective comics. He was so absorbed in Batman and Robin's confrontation with the Catwoman that he didn't notice Billy's restlessness. But all of a sudden, Billy couldn't tolerate the silence any longer. He grabbed the pillow from behind his head and threw it hard across the room at Jimmy. Jimmy dropped his comic and blocked the shot with both hands and laughed. He returned the pillow with identical force; only his aim wasn't so fortunate. The pillow missed Billy by at least a foot and hit the lamp on the nightstand instead, almost knocking it off. The lamp made a loud rattling noise.

"Oh my gosh," Billy exclaimed. "You are so lucky you didn't hit my signed eight by ten photo of Babe Ruth!"

"Um, it's a copy Billy. He didn't actually sign it."

"It don't matter you knucklehead" Billy started in. "The point is," Billy raised his voice, "you could have broken it."

"Well, even if I had hit it and broken it, you could just as easily pick yourself up another one down at the Delta General."

"Nuh-uh! They sold the last one a week ago Jimmy. Besides, I wouldn't be the one headin' there to buy it since I wouldn't have been the one who broke it."

"I don't know why you're so riled up anyway Billy. If you hadn't thrown the pillow at me in the first place, we wouldn't even be havin' this conversation about your precious little photo."

"It's an eight by ten, Jimmy. It ain't little."

"It's a fake! Who cares if it's as big as Goliath?"

"Who cares?!" Billy was appalled. "Jimmy, you're the biggest Babe Ruth fan I know!"

Jimmy didn't respond.

"Well, anyway, you got horrible aim Jimmy. You couldn't hit me if I was a donkey's ass." Had Billy known their mother was across the hall from their open attic door; he would have chosen to whisper the obscenity.

Ellen McGee had just finished checking on little Jordan, who was still napping, when the profanity exploded. She stopped in her tracks and stuck her head up into the attic stairwell.

Jimmy laughed. "You are a donkey's—" he started to say.

"You both had best be watchin' your tongues," Ellen warned with a firm whisper.

Jimmy and Billy looked wide-eyed at one another.

Mrs. McGee looked young for her age of thirty-eight, especially considering sixteen and a half of those years were spent raising her children. During three and a half of those years (1941-1944), she essentially parented Rose, Jimmy and Billy by herself while Tom

McGee had been overseas—first, with the 37th Engineer Battalion and later the 209th Engineer Combat Battalion. Ellen was a poised and gentle woman. She loved all four of her children dearly but she had no patience for foul language.

"And what was that noise all about?" Ellen wanted to know.

A slight pause was the boys' initial response. They looked at each other and then realized she must be talking about the rattling of the lamp. "Nothin'," they answered in unison.

"It was just my Ranger Rifle," Billy said. "It almost fell but I caught it."

"Uh-huh," Ellen doubted. "Just keep hushed. It took me long enough to get your little brother to sleep for the two of you to be makin' all that racket and wakin' him up."

"Yes ma'am," they answered.

"Thank Heavens you know how to fib. I'd be gettin' the switch if I'd have broke that lamp," Jimmy whispered. "Now all's you gotta do is learn how to watch your mouth," he laughed.

"Me?" Billy objected. "You curse all the time."

"Shh! Will you keep it down?"

"Why? The whole point is to make noise."

"Yeah, but not for you to tell the whole house that I curse," Jimmy clarified.

"Oh, sorry," Billy apologized. "I don't know why she's complainin' anyhow? The lamp didn't make that much noise."

"I think she just likes complainin'," concluded Jimmy.

"I think all moms do."

Jimmy got up and walked over to pick up Billy's pillow. Throughout their entire lives these identical twin brothers had always had one another's back. Even in their crib days, if one was hungry or thirsty or needed a change of diapers, it was often the other who made the announcement. Appearance-wise, there was not even a birthmark of a difference to distinguish the two boys, so Jimmy took it upon himself to make life easier for everyone by never leaving home without wearing his blue Brooklyn Dodgers baseball cap. They each stood five feet tall, an average height for their age, and weighed one hundred pounds. They had their father's bright blue eyes and their mother's silky brown hair. Their faces were tan from spending most of their free time outdoors.

Personality-wise, James Thomas McGee and William Jefferson McGee were clearly individuals. Jimmy was named after his Great Uncle Jim, a decorated WWI veteran. The twins adored Uncle Jim because he had always treated them as adults. He also had an exceptional memory for details so story-telling time with Great Uncle Jim was always a treat!

Jimmy was exactly eleven minutes older than his brother and anyone who knew them, knew that. In his mind, that made him smarter than Billy, and so Jimmy was determined to show others how he used judgment and logic in everything he did. Jimmy was the quieter of the two. He was a thinker and always gave careful thought before making choices. Every day the twins had chores and Jimmy made sure his were done correctly the first time around to avoid being scolded and forced to do them again.

Named after nobody in particular, Billy was dynamically carefree and constantly craved adventure. Risk and spontaneity drove his persona. Once, when Billy was seven, and going through his "I wonder what would happen if I . . ." stage, he nearly killed himself while testing out his envisioned flying abilities by jumping off the kitchen porch roof. He figured if the man from the comic book could do it, then why not give it a shot. So he painted a big red "S" on the front of one of his white T-shirts, tied a red tablecloth around his neck and jumped. Thank Heavens Mrs. McCrosky, from next door, was such a nosey neighbor. Eight weeks and zero chores later, Billy had fifty or more autographs on his cast and had come to the conclusion that the bragging rights he had reaped from his leap had been well worth its failed execution. Mrs. McCrosky had also been the first to witness flames coming out of the twins' older sister Rose's bedroom window one hot summer afternoon when Billy decided to get even with Rose for her tattling addiction by taunting her with a lit match held beneath her curtains. Much to his surprise, the tiny flame jumped up into the fabric and began engulfing the entire left side of the window. That little stunt earned Billy ten lashes from their daddy's switch.

"Hey Jimmy. Come over here and look at this! Quick!" A tiny drip of clear snot had crept to the edge of Billy's right nostril. It was dangling there, free as could be.

Jimmy looked up from beyond the pages of his Detective comic. "What?"

"I've had this little drip of snot hangin' from my nose for almost a whole minute now. Come look!"

Jimmy rolled his eyes. "You better not be gettin' sick. We need you to play baseball."

"I ain't gettin' sick Jimmy," Billy assured him. "I never get sick."

"Are you gonna wipe it off? It can't hang there forever."

"What if it did? What if I managed to keep this single drop here on my nose all day long? Imagine what people would say!"

"They'd say you're disgustin'. Now wipe it off!"

Billy sighed and wiped it away with his right hand. "You're no fun, Jimmy."

Billy then felt all around his neck and jawline. He was expecting to discover facial hair. After weeks of anticipation, the twins were looking in earnest for signs that would prove to the world they were finally becoming men. Their active imaginations had convinced them that becoming a teenager was magically accompanied by a host of overnight physical transformations that would catapult their bodies into a fledging display of manhood. So far, these dreams were turning out to be nothing but disappointments.

"Hey Jimmy, you got any stubble yet?"

Jimmy felt his face. "No, not yet," he said with a disappointed sigh. "Maybe tomorrow."

"To heck with that, I'm ready to slap some Palmolive on my face and get to shavin' today! All the other older boys in school are doin' it. What about zits? You got any zits?"

"I hope not, I don't want no zits."

5

"Well, I don't either but at least it'd be something." Billy laid there restless and then continued, "How tall you think we're gonna get? We should measure ourselves."

Just then, a single black Ked tennis shoe came flying through their wide-open, east bedroom window and onto the attic floorboards.

"Skip!" Billy announced with a huge smile and jumped up from his bed. He knew their friend Skip would come through with his part in the plan for them to get out of the house. Billy had hoped Skip's shoe landing on the attic floorboards might wake Jordan. But it didn't.

Skip Jones was fourteen and in charge. Although old enough to drive, but not old enough to smoke, Skip enjoyed the occasional indulgence of both. His birth name was Denny Jones, but he only responded to Skip and his wisdom on life made him the envy of all his friends. They thought it was neat how Skip got to do adult things like not have a curfew and cook his own meals and miss church. He even read the Sunday morning paper! Life was Skip's playground and no adult was ever going to convince him otherwise.

Skip's unexpected road to independence began on a dreadful Sunday evening at the age of nine when his parents were both killed in a horrible car wreck driving home from a Sunday company picnic. If Skip hadn't been invited to spend the afternoon at a friend's house, he'd be dead too. Grandpa Jones was Skip's only relative in town and what he knew about raising kids could be inscribed upon the tip of one of his Black and Mild cigars. Knowing this, Mrs. McCrosky offered to take guardianship immediately after the car accident, but Skip's proud grandfather thought she was too meddling and wouldn't allow it.

Billy hurried over to the east window. He stuck his head out and waved at Skip and returned his shoe. Skip stood five inches taller than the twins with a slight build. He had blue eyes with brown lashes. His short, sandy-blonde hair, which curled at its ends, was never combed.

Billy grabbed both he and Jimmy's baseball mitts from their desk beside the east window and hurried over to the stairwell. On his way, he tossed over Jimmy's mitt and Jimmy caught it.

"Mama," Billy called out so his voice would carry downstairs. He turned and winked at Jimmy and then leaned over the railing and called for her a second time and then a third. That's when their little brother Jordan began to stir awake.

Ellen was downstairs when she suddenly heard Billy's third call followed by the sounds of Jordan waking up. Now she was mad. She came upstairs to the attic door and whispered loud and clear, "Didn't I just tell you two to hush up."

"Um, yeah, but we're bored."

"And why is Skip standin' in our yard?"

"I reckon he's bored too. Can he please come in?"

"No," Ellen objected. She started to head downstairs hoping Jordan would fall back to sleep but instead he started wailing. He was now awake. Ellen gave out a long sigh of defeat. At this point, she just wanted the twins out of the house so she could try and get Jordan back to his nap. "Fine, the two of you's quietly tip-toe yourselves out of this house but I want you both home no less than a half hour before supper. Is that understood?"

Billy turned and gave his brother a big smile. "See Jimmy, I told you if we made enough noise during Jordan's nap she'd kick us out! Now come on! Let's go!"

2

With Mississippi Delta temperatures like these, there wasn't much else for a body to do but sit on the ol' front porch and wait for that afternoon breeze. Lyrics and news from Philco radios drifted along wrap-around porches and out into a wandering maze of giant oak tree branches draped with grey Spanish moss among the chandeliering tassels of the weeping willows. Winston Churchill's declaration of a "cold war" was all the nation's talk but on this Southern God-fearing afternoon it was the only reference to any sort of chill. In fact, the fevered air was so drenched with humidity that Lucifer himself would have prayed for rain.

Jimmy, Billy, and their friend Skip cut through wide and well-shaded front and back yards to where Whitey Greenburg lived. The Greenburg's house was the only single story home in town, except for those in the nearby all-Negro community of "Slytown." Mr. Greenburg lost his job with National Harvester last year, due to some structural setbacks. Because this forced the family to cut back expenses, they sold their huge plantation home on Bellflower and moved to Green Valley Drive.

Whitey, a bright-eyed towhead, mirrored the same enthusiasm for adventure as Billy. His favorite memory of their collaborated mischief was on the night of a fifth grade spelling bee in Mrs. Kinch's class when Billy slipped Whitey a frog from his pants pocket, that he subsequently placed on Alice Foster's shoulder while she was busy butchering the word "lieutenant." It wasn't but a moment before poor Alice noticed her new companion and erupted with panic. Both boys were taken straight home by their daddies and rendered a few lashes with the switch.

Whitey was doing nothing on the front porch when the boys came by. As soon as he was okay'd to leave, he hurried off with the boys to their next stop: Phillip Tupper's house. The fastest way there was to cut through Widow Hayes's yard. Pearl Hayes was a chatterbox whose husband had died of pneumonia two years prior. With her son and daughter-in-law living behind her and her three sisters Ruby, Opal and Sapphire one street away, the boys could never comprehend what fueled the widow's inclination to pay them so much attention. Nonetheless, she was a caring, elderly woman who perhaps knew the Bible better than any pastor in town.

As the boys stepped onto the green grass they could hear the Widow Hayes's voice welcoming them from the front porch of her antebellum home.

"How'do boys!" Mrs. Hayes was sitting in her wicker rocking chair and looking quite "art deco" in her old flower print summer dress while waving a fan about her face.

"Hi there, Mrs. Hayes!" they responded cordially.

"Does she ever leave that chair?" Billy whispered.

When the Widow Hayes asked where the boys were off to, she was appalled to hear they'd even consider such activities on a hot day like this. As she rambled on she revealed that "Phillip" was "inside her parlor right now fixin' a loose leg of one of my sittin' chairs. I'd fix it myself, of course, but these bones of mine are gettin' so's I can't do much of nothing like that no more. I'm just not as able as I use to be," she explained.

Even though she carried on listing her incapacities, followed by a random tangent about considering herself a "Mississippian" above an American, the boys heard no further than the part about Phillip Tupper working.

On a laziness scale of one to ten (with ten being the laziest), Phillip Tupper would rank somewhere around an eleven. His mother attributed this to him being overweight with sloping shoulders. Every day she tried to get him on a diet, swearing she could not bear to see her only son grow up to become "a glutton." Philly figured with all the exercise he got playing baseball every day, why worry. After all, the only results he ever noticed from all the diets were feelings of starvation. Over the past year, the boys had grown so tired of Philly's whining that they responded by sneaking him food from their homes so he'd hush up.

"We gotta see this!" Whitey gleamed.

"May we speak with him for a moment ma'am?" Skip asked the Widow Hayes, interrupting her rambling.

"Uh, well, um, I don't see why not. Go right on in boys. Make yourselves at home. Would y'all care for some sweet tea?"

"No thanks," the boys declined as they headed onto the deep porch, with its massive and high pillars, and stepped inside. Before reaching the parlor they were greeted by the widow's smiling housemaid Sissy, a rail-thin black woman on her way to delivering the widow her afternoon glass of sweet tea. Sissy directed the boys to the parlor where they found their red-haired friend at the far end of the room twisted up underneath an elegant-looking chair.

At first, the boys, with their satisfied expressions, kept silent. They weren't about to interrupt Philly until they had extracted some enjoyment from the view.

Finally, Skip announced their presence "Hey boy!"

Philly jerked his head up and knocked it against the bottom of the chair.

"Ouch! What the heck?!" Philly scrambled to pry himself out from under the chair. "Why you boys gotta come up and scare me like that? Darn near gave me a heart attack Skip!" he whimpered, while nervously rubbing his nose with his palm, a rather repulsive habit that no one understood. Everyone in the room was laughing by now. Philly looked around at all his friends with a pouty expression.

"What're you boys up to in there?" asked the Widow Hayes, curious about the noise.

"Uh, nothin' ma'am." Philly hesitated. "Y'all are gonna get me in trouble. I came to help Mrs. Hayes, not fiddle around." Philly wiped the beads of sweat off of his brow and onto his pant leg.

"Well, how close are you to bein' done cause we're on way to the diamond for some baseball," said Jimmy.

"In this heat? No way!" Philly refused. "It's too hot to play baseball."

"You always say that Philly and you always play," Whitey pointed out.

Philly whimpered and wiped the sweat from his brow. "A body can get sick in this heat."

The boys all rolled their eyes.

"Waitaminute. How'd you two get permission to play ball today?" Philly asked the twins.

"Because I came up with a genius plan and it worked!" Billy commended himself.

"Well Happy Birthday boys," Philly acknowledged.

Jimmy and Billy nodded in appreciation. "This heat ain't gonna kill you Philly, now come on!" Jimmy was about to saddle up and deliver a long-winded speech about friendship and loyalty before Philly put a stop to it by giving in.

After tightening a few more loose screws, Philly reported the completion of his work to the Widow Hayes. He then took off with his friends to their next destination: the stately, three-story, Victorian home of Harold "Fist" Bradshaw II that stood across the street and down a long driveway.

Harold was terribly short for his age and had a hard time forgetting about it. To compensate, he posed as a tough guy to ward off those who believed his height made him a target for name-calling. Last summer, Harold's mother forced him to join the church choir with high hopes of her only son becoming the next Mr. Bing Crosby. Harold hated singing anyway, but despised this all the more because it involved public display.

On Harold's Sunday morning debut, his friends watched from the pews, chuckling under their breaths as Harold stood in silence among the choir. It was such an awkward sight with Harold being the only kid up there and refusing to open his mouth at all. Still, it earned him nicknames like "choir boy" and "Harold the

Harmonizer." He scowled at them all and overnight transformed his entire image. He started dressing like all the older boys. His overalls were replaced with slacks and his button down shirts were left unbuttoned over T's and tank tops. His older cousin Bobby even gave his light brown haired mop a GI haircut. It was a nice try but still failed when a couple of tenth graders mocked Harold's haircut and pointed out that his wrinkled brow looked more like rows in a farmer's field. Everyone outside of Harold's friends broke into fits of laughter. "Cornfield" was thoroughly disgraced and to prove his virility, he tightened up his right hand and socked both boys square in the nose. Everyone just stood there; speechless with wide eyes and dropped jaws. Perhaps even more unexpected were the looks of fear on the two victims' faces. Harold's new legacy was forever etched into history and that very next day, "Fist" picked two fights: one with a brand new boy in school whose family had just moved into town and the other with a willow tree branch that Fist swore had tapped him on the shoulder. Fist was proud of his new self, finally seeing a light at the end of the dark tunnel that had characterized his previous existence of being surrounded by four sisters (and no brothers) who had always adored pinching his cheeks and calling him their "little sweetheart" in public.

Jimmy hurried up to the grand front porch and rapped on the screen door. Mrs. Bradshaw came forth looking as pretty as always. She informed the boys that Harold was upstairs in his bedroom and invited them in. On their way up the monstrous staircase, they could already hear their friend Vincent DiVincenzo's dreadful Yankee accent. Vincent was an only child from the North End of Boston, Massachusetts. The company Mr. DiVincenzo worked for was growing and a generous promotion relocated the family to Mississippi. Although his office was in the city of Vicksburg, he liked the small-town feel of Eugene and moved the family there just in time for Vincent to begin the third grade.

Vincent's mouth was even more assertive than Fist's and he was only ever referred to by the nickname "Boston".

Boston and Fist were both eleven and a half years old and inseparable. Boston was three inches taller than Fist, and just as skinny. Oddly enough, the difference in height did not bother Fist one bit. Being a Southerner still made him immeasurably superior to any Yankee.

When the boys reached the top of the stairs, they found these two best friends seated together Indian-style on Fist's bedroom floor amongst a collage of baseball cards arguing.

"Done! I am done! You're killing me here Fist!" Boston rushed to his feet and paced once before heading over to Fist's dresser. Sitting on top of it was Boston's shoebox of baseball cards. "This is ridiculous and I'll tell you what else," Boston snatched up his shoebox and turned around to face Fist. "It's not about your '31 Gomez being a whole decade older than my Reese. It's about the fact that it's Pee Wee Reese's rookie card I got here. You know anyone else who has it?" Boston had removed the lid to his shoebox and was rummaging through it. Whatever he was searching for, it seemed, wasn't there because ten seconds later he was seated back on the floor in front of Fist. He acknowledged the other boys with a double nod as if they had been standing there all day. "Just 'cause your Gomez card is older don't make it worth more to me. Reese ain't up for grabs Fist and that's all there is to it."

Fist stared at Boston with an annoyed expression.

"Exactly. That's what I thought. You got nothing to say. So just forget it. I'm not giving up Reese." Boston's thick, dark hair and brown eyes came from his one hundred percent Italian background.

"Well then, here's my 1941 'Chuck' Klein and my George Case." Fist expectantly offered both together in one hand and reached out to claim Reese's rookie.

"No, no, no!" Boston snatched up his prize possession. "Are you guys seeing this?" he asked the other boys. "You've got to be fooling me Fist Bradshaw."

"What about my Feller?"

Boston quickly shook his head no.

"Hubbell?"

"Did I not just say this conversation was done?" Boston went to stand up but stopped himself with a thought that appeared to impress him. "But I will trade you my Double Play of Herman and Hack for your Gomez."

"Oh no you won't. This is a 1931 Lefty Gomez, you don't just give it up for nothin'."

"Alright then, forget it. We're done."

"Fine." Fist paused for a brief moment. "Hold on. I change my mind. You can have my Lefty Gomez," he said. "But I want your Ted Williams."

"Are you nuts?!" Boston ridiculed. "Why would I give up a player's card from my home team?"

Just then, Whitey stepped in. "Hey Boston, give him your Ty Cobb and call it even."

Boston turned and drove a look into Whitey's soul. "You're just as nuts as he is! That's my dad's card. He'd whip me if I traded it."

"Well then, how about my Joe Cronin rookie?" Fist suggested.

"1933?"

"Yep."

"How'd you get that?"

Fist walked over to his bed. Hanging on the wall beside it was a small shelf. Sitting on top of the shelf was a small wooden box. Inside the box was Joe Cronin's rookie card. Fist sat back down in front of Boston and waived the card before Boston's wide-open eyes. Fist had no intention of actually giving up Cronin's rookie card. It was all part of a bait and switch.

"Fine." Boston finally agreed and handed over his Pee Wee Reese rookie card.

Fist switched Cronin's card with Feller's and attempted to hand it over to Boston.

"What's that?" Boston wanted to know.

"What's what? This? Um, it's the card I'm about to trade you."

"Oh, no, no, no, no, no! We agreed to Cronin not Feller." Boston couldn't spat off the word "no" just once. "Forget the whole thing,

Fist. I'm not trading with you if you're going to try and be a crook about it."

"Why would you not want Feller? Joe Dimaggio even said no one will ever out throw him," argued Fist.

"And he also said his curveball wasn't human-like." Billy added.

"Nobody asked you Billy McGee," said Boston. "Fist, we're done. I'm not givin' up Reese and that's final."

Fist stood up and glared down at his friend who was still seated on the floor.

"What are you planning on doing?" Boston scoffed.

"Stand up and I'll show you," Fist challenged.

"Oh my Lord, he's gonna blow a fuse," Jimmy said under his breath.

Finally, Skip spoke up. "Alright you two. Before one of you hotheads snaps your cap—that's enough! Look, we came here to play some baseball. So why don't we all go fetch Charlie and get to goin' already."

Jimmy pointed out that the afternoon was already underway and they wouldn't have much time to play if they continued squandering it over a pointless argument. It took about five minutes of convincing but finally Boston and Fist called a truce.

Like sheep, Skip herded everyone down the stairs and out the front door over to Charlie Blair's house. Mr. and Mrs. Blair were on their wrap around porch enjoying some shade with their two year-old, son Clayton. They told the boys that Charlie had been sent to Schnook's' on a quick shopping errand and the boys politely gave their thanks and hurried off down Green Valley Drive into town.

Nestled in a quiet cove a few miles northeast of where the Mississippi and Big Black Rivers intersect lays the drowsy little bayou town of Eugene, Mississippi. One hundred and thirty years ago, two newlywed couples settled along the backwaters of this region and built a sturdy little gristmill. They were the Eugene brothers from LeFleur's Bluff, Mississippi. The brother's new venture thrived and soon fueled the birth of a new town in their name. The two couples each gave birth to sons, which they had

hoped would eventually take over the family business. Thirty
years later, in 1849, the Eugene cousins packed up their families
and headed west for gold country. They did well for themselves and
both cousins urged their parents to sell the family gristmill and join
them in California. The Eugene brothers, now over the age of sixty,
agreed.

Although the gristmill business floundered under its new
ownership, with two intersecting rivers and a foundation of rich
soil, the town of Eugene continued to grow into five brick streets,
now adorned with blooming magnolia trees, and a shoulder-to-
shoulder assembly of two and three-story small businesses. Union
Boulevard is the main drag. Its red and white-striped awnings and
shingled overhangs complimented the flower boxes that garnished
the second and third-story checkrail windows, which advertised the
names of businesses. A single, wide, dirt road, named Portage Trail,
moseyed away from the town and roved for miles until arriving at
the next and nearest sign of life: a large river-city, twelve miles to
the northeast, named Vicksburg.

As the well-shaded Green Valley Drive led the boys into town,
where they first passed the filling station managed by Fist's uncle.
Fist's uncle was off that day but his son Dale was working. Dale
waved to the boys from his rocking chair below the Gulf 15 cents
a gallon sign. Schnook's Grocery was the largest store on the
block. Without going in, the boys could see Charlie through the
front display windows. They rapped on the glass until they caught
Charlie's attention. His crystal blue eyes smiled with the anticipation
of baseball as he waved for his friends to come inside.

Charlie Blair always looked like he stepped right off a
Hollywood movie screen. He was thirteen but looked a year; maybe
two, older with dark hair, perfect skin, a perfect tan and perfectly
dark eyelashes. As he knew it, Charlie might have been second to
Skip, in height, but, in terms of vanity, he was second to no one.

As the seven boys romped into the store, Fess and Leland, the
afternoon clerks, became nervous. They were sure that the boys

would be a bother to their quiet customers, so Fess headed right for them with his finger pressed to his lips.

Charlie first had to run home and drop off the tin of Johnson's wood floor cleaner to his mother. The other boys continued through town to the baseball diamond.

At the next block, Billy let out a gigantic sigh. "Oh Lord, why is this town so boring? I can't stand it here."

Jimmy turned his head and looked at his brother with a dampened spirit. He did not feel the same. "Lighten up, will ya. It ain't that bad."

"Are you kidding me? Take a look around. There ain't nothing ever goin' on here. It's pathetic."

With this comment, Whitey tapped the back of Billy's head and challenged him to a race to the baseball diamond. Billy accepted the challenge and off they went. The other boys followed suit and in no time they had all arrived.

Jefferson Davis School was the largest building in town and the boys' beautiful baseball diamond was located directly behind it. The schoolhouse was two solid stories of red brick with two feet of visible cement foundation. A wide cement staircase led up to the arched main entrance with its double doors. Across the entire front and back of the structure were factory windows. On opposite ends of its roof rose two black double brick chimneys. Altogether, it was an impressive-looking, well-built structure.

A sliver of the ball field was visible from the street and for these boys, each time seeing it felt like their first. Their eyes grew big and their hearts began to beat faster with anticipation. Years ago, Charlie's uncle was the school janitor and he and Charlie's dad would take Charlie and his older brother Clint there as kids. They taught the two boys everything they knew about batting, pitching, catching and fielding. As Charlie became old enough to actually play he convinced every boy, his age, in town that since his uncle was the school janitor this gave him carte blanche to claim the diamond for himself. After all, his uncle maintained the school's property, both inside and out, so that meant all rights belonged to the Blair's. Charlie, of course, needed a team in order to play, so he invited his friends and uninvited everyone around his age. Henceforth, the boys considered the diamond to be their own private sanctuary. The only time they could not use it was on some Friday nights when the men's church league played and at lunchtime during the school year, when the High School boys used it. The ball field embodied everything they could ever dream of, from its regulation dimensions and home run fence to its sturdy backstop and elevated pitchers mound. There was even a bench to the left of the backstop for a dugout and behind this there were some bleachers. Beyond the diamond's outfield were woods that stretched for a mile or two before turning into bayou swampland.

The boys were lucky to have such a first-class facility in their small Mississippi town, so they were mindful of its upkeep.

Altogether, there were nine boys in the group. With only enough boys for one team, Skip had designed an advancing rotation system that allowed everyone to play each position. But this left the defense one man short because someone was always at bat, so Jimmy and Skip decided that it made the most sense to only have two players cover he outfield. On the rare occasion that their friend T.J. was not able to sneak away from Slytown to play with the white boys, the shortstop position was eliminated from the rotation and the second baseman was responsible for covering both areas. Most of the time, this wasn't an issue, but once in a while if certain white folk were not minding their own business, certain situations were likely to arise. Fortunately, for T.J. the boys always stood up for him.

Once the batter; either got a hit, struck out, or drew a walk, he would then assume first base and become the new first baseman and each player would then advance to their next assigned position. And this continued just like clockwork. Skip and Jimmy also made sure that each day's playing order was arranged so that Billy, with his natural pitching arm, was on the mound every time Jimmy, the star hitter, was at bat. This way, Jimmy could polish up on his batting skills. Jimmy had remarkable control over his swing and could send most hits pretty much anywhere necessary. It was amazing to watch.

Billy was known for his pitching, particularly his curveball. It was so wild and crazy that it even posed a serious challenge to Jimmy's swing. Billy had exceptional control over this pitch. Whenever it first left Billy's hand, it was so wide it appeared to be heading straight for the batter. About three-quarters of the way from the mound to the batter's box, the ball began veering inward and at the last moment, made a sharp turn and fell perfectly within the strike zone. The batter would be so worried about getting hit that his swing would either be delayed or off stride every time.

After one complete rotation, Charlie appeared from the woods with a skinny twelve-year-old black boy wearing blue overalls and a gray hound's tooth cap at his side. The boy's full name was Tyrone Jackson but everyone knew him as "T.J."

T.J. was the only black person the boys knew, other than those employed in Eugene. He was brought into the group through Skip, who knew him first. The two of them had met just after Skip's parents died and Skip was spending a lot of time roaming the woods alone to clear his head. T.J. was a good listener and Skip needed that, so the two bonded right away.

As the boys played ball, the twins tried their best to pay attention to the position of the afternoon sun so they would not be late for their birthday supper. When the afternoon breeze finally came, it felt sweet and cool against everyone's sweaty faces and Jimmy and Billy both looked up into the clear, blue sky that reached out forever. They then looked at one another and smiled. They were blessed to have each other. Although they bickered from time to time, overall, they couldn't imagine a happier life and a better way to spend their thirteenth birthday. After a few full rotations, a loud movement came from the woods beyond the outfield. Without a second glance, T.J. said a hasty goodbye and disappeared.

From the woods, ten threadbare juveniles came sauntering into the ball field, some with hats worn sideways and others were biting on the ends of toothpicks. Leading this band of outcasts was a 5'6" tall, chesty, fourteen-year-old boy, wearing a brown, tweed Peebles cap and a sour expression.

Jimmy was standing next to Skip. He leaned in and said with disgust, "Why are they here?"

Skip drew in a deep sigh. "You know why they're here Jimmy."

"Yeah," Jimmy sighed. "I reckon I do."

3

Jonas King was charmed with looks but not with character. The dark, kinky-haired and olive-skinned renegade was known throughout Eugene for his antagonistic behavior and rude conduct. The boys had always referred to Jonas and his associates as "the mob," a suitable title for a group of their stature. The mob had been crossing paths with the boys since grade school and the boys had yet to recall a pleasant encounter. Jonas's dominant personality and age made him the gang's unofficial leader. Collectively, they disturbed the peace and played baseball.

Like an old western showdown, the mob stopped short of the boys, who were prepared with their chests out, chins up and various threatening expressions on their faces. Skip stood in front of his boys, glare to glare with Jonas. Each leader waited for the other to open the floor.

Finally, Skip spoke. "Jonas," he said, with a nod of his head.

Jonas nodded back without a single word.

Skip paused a moment before asking: "What are you boys doin' here?"

Before answering, Jonas took off his cap and ran his hands through his dark waves of hair. He then switched the cap around, so the bill faced back, and made sure it was secure.

"Well," he began, "you know that old empty lot me and my boys have been usin' for a ball field'? It's owned by some fella who lives over yonder in Vicksburg and we just got word he's gonna be movin' down here and buildin' himself a house right there on that empty lot." Jonas paused and sniffed his nose before continuing. "So, we was figurin' since this here school belongs to everyone—not just y'all—we got just as equal right to use this diamond ourselves. After all, it is public property."

At first, the boys just stood there in angry silence. This was not the first time the mob had presented an argument for taking over the baseball diamond before.

"Your uncle ain't been the janitor for almost a year now," Jonas said to Charlie. "So we ain't fallin' for that bullshit line of yours no more."

"Alright then." Skip immediately responded. He then thought for a moment before continuing. "You got yourselves a deal. We'll share the diamond."

With this, the jaws of each one of Skip's friends dropped to the ground in utter horror.

Jonas began stroking the unshaved stubble below his chin. "Well, you see that's the thing. Seein' how y'all have been usin' this diamond for the past, oh, what's it been, three or four years now abouts, we figured it was about time y'all just gave it up and let us have it."

"Waitaminute," Charlie spoke up. "If it's public property, then how can you say you's get to have it?"

"Exactly. That's why we'll share it," Skip reiterated plainly. "You and your boys can use it half of the week and we'll take it the other half."

This was not the point Charlie was trying to establish. He looked to Jimmy for some help, but Jimmy was speechless.

"I don't think your gettin' what I'm tryin' to say here Skip." Jonas's complacent tone switched to one of impatience. "We got no interest in sharin' the diamond with you boys. We want it all summer long, all day long, for ourselves. Got it?"

Skip shifted his weight to one side and his hands began to fidget about. Their movement was distracting his concentration so he tried hard to keep them still. As this only got worse, Skip pushed them into his back pockets.

"Now, I hope you and your boys have enjoyed yourselves this afternoon, but seein' how the diamond's now ours—" Jonas began.

"You're crazy if you think we're gonna give this up!" Whitey warned and nervously adjusted his lucky St. Louis Cardinals cap that he always wore.

"Sounds to me like they're just lookin' for an ass woopin'," Fist challenged. "I'll stomp every single one of 'em Skip. Just let me at 'em!"

"Me too!" Boston joined in.

"Both of you's, put a sock in it," Skip muttered over his shoulder.

"Look at Jonas," Fist whispered to Boston. "He acts like he's God or something."

"What was that Harold?" Jonas clearly heard Fist's comment and poked his head up and around Skip's so he could get a clear view of the boy.

"I said—" Fist prepared to repeat his remark loud and clear.

"Fist! Enough!" Skip scolded.

"You've got to be kidding me," Boston sided with Fist and said under his breath. "What? So we're not allowed to talk right now?"

Skip debated whether he should turn around to respond to Boston's gripe or do so with both eyes remaining fixed on Jonas. He chose the latter of the two. "Exactly! Don't talk!"

Boston was never any good at biting his tongue. He, along with everyone else wanted to know why these boys thought they could just show up and in one swift move declare the diamond as their own without a fight. The boys had all seen the tragic condition of the empty lot on Locust Street where the mob played. Not only was it always filled with trash, one of the neighbors allowed his dogs to potty there. But if the mob took over the diamond that empty lot would be the only other available space in town where the boys could play ball. But, as Jonas mentioned, it was soon to be developed. And Skip's arbitrary surrender to share the baseball diamond was far from appreciated by his friends.

Jimmy stepped forward and stood beside Skip with his game face on. The others boys followed Jimmy's lead. Skip looked off into the distance for a brief moment and smiled as if he was laughing inside. He then glared at Jonas.

"So what now?" Skip began in a cold tone. "We're just supposed to step back and let you fellas have this field all to yourselves? We've been through this before with y'alls. So you's already oughta know that we ain't givin'up this diamond for nothin'."

"Too bad," stated Jonas, and the mob nodded their agreement practically in unison.

Skip looked as though he was ready to pound Jonas right between the eyes. Skip's gaze returned to the ground and the muscles in his neck began tightening up. He so wanted to kick the crap out of Jonas right then and there and with his friends all behind for support, the option was viciously tempting. However, Skip managed to maintain his composure by drawing in one sharp breath. Besides, fighting would only set a bad example to the others.

When Skip was ready to speak, he spoke. "I take it back then. We won't share it."

"That's exactly right, 'cause we're now takin' over," Jonas accepted.

"That's it!" Fist threatened and sprang forward with both hands clenched.

"Fist!" Skip warned. "Will somebody please calm him down?"

This made the mob laugh. "Just what are you plannin' on doin' there chicken?" Lil' Denny mocked.

"I'll tear you up Lil' Denny," threatened Fist.

"Fist, I said, knock it off!" Skip snapped.

The mob all broke into a fit of laughter.

"What shorty? Is Skip now your mother too?" Lil' Denny prodded at Fist.

Fist charged at the mob again but Skip held him back. Meanwhile, Skip took notice of a sheepish-looking character in the background of the mob boys. He had never seen this face before and there was something peculiar about the boy.

"Who exactly you calling shorty, you midget?!" Boston yelled over Skip's head to defend Fist. Lil' Denny was oddly short for his twelve years. "I hear that's why you keep getting held back in school?"

"That, along with being a fat-head like the rest of 'em," Philly chuckled.

"Fat-head? How long has it been since your last pancake breakfast there fat-ass!" scoffed Jonas's right-hand man Sampson.

"Yeah, and it looks like you just took first place in a pie eating contest too, you tub o' lard!" mocked Dale.

Philly's expression became enraged.

"Oh yeah? You think we're just gonna stand here and take this?!" Fist clamored, while Whitey and Billy worked to hold him back.

Sampson stepped forward with lethal brown eyes and flared nostrils.

"You wanna tough me?" Fist challenged and right away both boys drew their fists back.

"Alright. Let's go! Right here! You and me Small Fry!" Sampson accepted.

"Yeah. I'd like to see that," Morgan joined in.

Fist was about to explode into a blazing ball of kicking and swinging, but Charlie reached forward and stopped him cold with a tight grip on his arm.

"Uh-huh, that's what I thunk," said Jonas.

"Um, its thought, Jonas, not thunk," Glenn Parker corrected. Jonas responded to his friend with an annoyed glare.

But Fist wasn't done yet. He squeezed free of Charlie's grip and continued on. "You with me Boston?"

"Let's do it!" Boston stepped directly forward with a threatening scowl.

"That's enough!" Skip ordered to Boston and Fist. "No one's fightin' nobody here. Not today, at least," Skip established. "And . . ." he turned to face Jonas and the mob. "There ain't no way in hell we're givin' up this here diamond. That just ain't fair. So y'all better forget about the whole idea."

The mob boys didn't move.

"Go on now," Skip tried to shoo them away like mice.

Jonas remained still with both feet planted in the dirt. His counterparts did the same. After taking a deep breath, Jonas said, "Alright then, you wanna be fair. I can do that. But if we're gonna be fair that means only one thing."

Skip was loosely curious.

"That means we play for it," stated Jonas.

"What d'you mean, play for it?" Jimmy questioned.

Jonas drew in a long, deep breath. "Well, Jimmy, that was actually another idea we've been discussin'. The only proper way to really decide on who gets a baseball diamond is to play baseball. Whoever wins the game, wins the diamond; plain and simple."

"Hmm," Skip shook his head.

"If you boys need time to discuss we understand," Jonas's sneering tone made it seem as though some sinister plot was already up his grungy sleeve.

"Hey Skip," Jimmy whispered. "Why not talk it over? Maybe this ain't such a bad idea," Jimmy tried to whisper but all his friends heard.

Jimmy searched around for his friends' opinions. It was obvious by the uneasy silence that this was too big of a decision to make without properly discussing it first. So Skip gathered them into a tight huddle.

Fist was the first to speak. "Why don't we forget all about playin' and just pound their butts like I suggested in the first place!"

"Fine. And then we can all get thrown in jail," Skip pointed out.

"We can't get arrested for fightin'," argued Whitey.

"Wanna bet? It's called disturbin' the peace," Skip stated.

"So what are you thinkin' right now Skip?" Charlie was curious to know.

"Honestly, I'm not too sure about this whole idea."

"Why not?" Philly pleaded. "We got the best pitcher, slugger, infielder, and outfielder in town right here."

"Philly's right," Billy concurred. "This here's an opportunity of a lifetime to finally keep them mob boys from always comin' over here and tryin' to take over."

"I know, but let's think about something here. Why else would they seem so suddenly eager to challenge us unless they was certain about winnin'?" Skip wondered. "Something fishy's goin' on. I don't know exactly what it is? I mean, I like the idea but at the same time I don't. I think we definitely need some time to think about it."

"Hold on a minute," Whitey stepped in. "Is it just me or is there ten of them?"

The boys looked up and carefully counted the mob. Sure enough, just like Skip had noticed earlier there were ten boys. Someone new had joined the mob. Right away, the boys spotted the newcomer. None of them had ever seen this kid before.

"Hey," Boston called out. "Where'd that new kid come from? There's ten of you now and last time I checked a baseball team's only supposed to have nine."

"Don't worry none 'bout that. There'll only be nine of us playin'," answered Felix.

"Well, who is that fella wearin' the cap back there?" Philly asked, pointing to a sheepish lad in beige slacks and a faded madras shirt. A few strands of dark, curly, hair could be spotted hanging out from the small red cap.

"This here's our ball retriever. I guess you could call him our own personal servant," Jonas answered proudly.

"What's your name kid?" Skip called to him.

The stranger was too busy studying his feet to respond.

"We call him Slave," Sampson answered for him.

"Slave?! Are you kidding me?" Boston could hardly believe his ears. "Who the heck does that?" Boston shook his head in disgust and turned to make an exit. "This whole thing is ridiculous. I say we just forget it. Done! That's it! The diamond's ours."

"I'm with you Boston!" agreed Fist. "These boys are only gonna end up findin' a way of cheatin' us."

"Exactly," Boston agreed.

27

"They're right Skip. You know they're gonna do it," said Jimmy. "Plus, what are we gonna do about T.J.? He won't be safe on that field playin' against them mob boys but we need him to have nine."

Jimmy brought up an important dilemma. With this, the boys regrouped.

Skip took a slow deep breath. He thought quietly for a moment while the other boys each chimed in on top of Jimmy's concern. He knew they needed T.J.'s talents to help them win. Finally, Skip interrupted them and said, "I think there might be a way around both these issues." His tone had changed and was now quite confident.

While his friends quietly waited with rapt attention, Skip sank back into deep thought. "I might have a plan to keep them from bein' able to cheat, but I need to talk to a few people first. As for T.J., let me think about that a little bit more. But I'm pretty sure I can come up with a plan that'll keep him safe. So, do y'all trust me?" he asked the group.

Everyone, except Jimmy, nodded in agreement. Jimmy was changing his whole opinion about the game.

"Okay. Then it's settled. We play. And as for T.J., I will talk to him tomorrow."

"This is a bad idea Skip." Jimmy was shaking his head back and forth. "Bad for T.J."

"Jimmy, it'll be okay. T.J.'s a tough boy—tougher than you think. Besides, we need him to win and you know it. We can talk more about this later, but for now, are you in?"

Jimmy paused.

"Come on Jimmy," urged Billy. "You were just sayin' this game ain't such a bad idea. It'll be all right."

With a sigh, Jimmy reluctantly agreed.

The boys broke from their huddle and Skip sealed the deal with Jonas.

The game date was set for July fourth, which was a Friday and only two weeks away. Skip insisted on this date because although Friday evenings were when the men sometimes played, July fourth was the town's annual picnic so there was never a men's game. In addition, Skip knew this date could ensure a good turnout of spectators since all the stores in town closed by mid-afternoon for the holiday. So both groups concluded that it made sense for the game to be scheduled for mid-afternoon, and not interfere with the evening picnic.

Although most folks in town were bigots, Skip was hoping a sizeable attendance would help to ensure T.J's safety if things got out of control on the ball field. Certainly, enough of the adults in town would not want any trouble that might create drama between the white folks of Eugene and the black folks of Slytown if a young boy from their community was ever harmed.

The mob made their exit and Jimmy and Billy dashed off for home. Their intended first order of business was to head upstairs for a height check against their closet door but Ellen cut them off at the pass and sent them straight to the supper table.

The McGee residence was a modest and well-maintained structure that stood three stories high, including the walk-up attic. The front porch stretched across the entire front of the house. The house faced south. The porch was covered and outfitted with a pair of comfortable white rockers and a sturdy porch swing. The entire house and garage were painted with a sunbeam yellow, which was Ellen's favorite color. Once inside a rich dark-stained banister and staircase rose up from the modest foyer, stopped once at the landing and disappeared from sight. Two wide, arched openings, trimmed in mahogany opened off the foyer on the left and right. Each opening respectively gave view to the living room and to the parlor. The parlor was smaller than the living room, but its simplicity made it seem more spacious. More natural light entered this room, as there was no porch roof outside the two windows on its east wall. This light showed off its flowered-print walls of oil paintings and ornately framed family photos. This was the one room in the house where no amount of horseplay was allowed. Ellen strictly maintained its elegant appearance and made it clear on innumerable occasions that heads would surely roll if so much as one lace doily were ruffled.

The living room was darker, with richer tones from the mahogany trim. The windows were framed with long truffle rose taffeta draperies and sheer curtains that diffused the limited amount of sunlight that filtered in from the porch. In the center of the room was a sofa nestled between two end tables, facing a rocker and Tom's big green upholstered chair. This is where Tom sat every night after supper. He would read the newspaper to stay caught up on current events. In the southwest corner was a decoratively carved corner hutch. This displayed Ellen's elegant glassware and china that was used for company. Between the south-facing windows stood a tall drop-leaf desk and beside it sat a small, straight-back chair. The seat of the chair had a cushioned cover that was done in needlepoint. Whenever it was time to sort through the bills, Tom would move the seat in front of the desk and this was where he sat.

Another wide, wood-trimmed archway on the opposite side opened into the dining room. Four windows and a window seat spanned the length of its west wall. On it's north wall was a mahogany buffet that stored the everyday dishes. In the center of the room was an oval mahogany table surrounded by six chairs. There was a swinging door on its east wall that led into the kitchen. This was the brightest room in the house and although it was cluttered with all the necessary modern-day conveniences, Ellen kept it orderly and clean with Pine Sol.

Every week Ellen cleaned the furniture with a vinegar and water solution. On the first Friday of each month, she used a furniture polish to give the wood an extra shine.

The second floor had three bedrooms and a bath, with the largest bedroom belonging to Tom and Ellen.

Ellen had prepared a savory meal of fried chicken, field peas, mashed potatoes, and corn bread. The boys sat down as Ellen placed Jordan in his high chair and then along came their sixteen-year-old sister Rose wearing a haughty smirk on her face. Rose was becoming a beautiful young lady although some of her behaviors around the twins were still a bit juvenile. But Rose possessed a skill that no one else had ever entirely mastered: no matter what the circumstances, Rose could always tell these two identical twins apart. Even in their younger years of playing pranks by trading places, Rose always knew, without a doubt, which was Jimmy and which was Billy.

"Where have you two been?" Rose sneered. "I thought birthdays were supposed to be spent here with the family."

"That's none of your business now, is it," Billy snapped back.

Ellen gave Billy a stern look before going into the kitchen to fetch the pitcher of sun tea. That's when Tom came down from upstairs which prompted Rose to remark again on their absence. Jimmy reached over and yanked hard on her long, brown curls. "You're so annoying," he belittled

Tom proceeded to speak: "I know your Mama said you could leave with Skip, but she also said to be home a half hour ago. So would either one of you care to explain why you're late?"

Jimmy and Billy just sat there, knowing that no answer would satisfy him.

"Did y'all forget today was your birthday?" Tom accused.

"No sir," Billy began. "But we're all sittin' down at the same time, so . . . ?"

Tom felt Billy's remark was a shade too sarcastic and let him know it with a light smack on the back of his head.

"Honest Daddy, we was on our way to leavin' about an hour ago but Jonas and them fellas showed up and, well, they kinda wouldn't let us leave."

"Hmm," was all the more Tom had to say about the situation and Rose planted an unsatisfied expression on her face for the remainder of the meal.

Suppertime was generally characterized with Jimmy and Billy voraciously downing their food while Jordan picked at his. Ellen would try to coax him into eating it while Tom would discuss both local and worldly events and Rose, meanwhile, always tried to remain poised like the proper young lady she considered herself to be.

After a delicious meal, Whitey and his folks came over for birthday cake and ice cream with fresh blackberries. While the adults visited inside, Jimmy and Billy went out onto the front porch where they bragged to Whitey about Jordan's amazing ability to read at the ripe age of two. Though Jordan obviously couldn't read a lick, what he did possess was an extraordinary memory, so much that his little brain had actually memorized the sounds of every word that signaled the turn of a page in all three of his books. The twins nestled Jordan between them while Jimmy read aloud. Billy informed Whitey. "Now watch. He'll follow along with the words and when it's time to turn the page he will!" And he did! And Whitey was impressed.

The air was still thick and stubbornly humid but overall it was much more tolerable now that the sun was no longer beating down. When Jimmy finished reading, Jordan found bliss in a snail making his way across floorboards as Jimmy and Billy relaxed on the porch swing and Whitey on the porch railing. They groaned back and forth about that afternoon's encounter with the mob until Billy decided to change the subject. He asked Whitey, "Hey, I got a question for ya. You shavin' yet?"

Whitey shook his head no. Then there was silence. Jimmy was about to ask a question of his own but Whitey spoke up first. He lowered his voice to make sure his words wouldn't carry beyond the twins' ears. "Do y'all um, does your, uh . . ." Whitey was having a real difficult time spitting out his inquiry. "Does your thing ever stick straight up?"

Jimmy and Billy both looked at each other waiting for the other to answer first.

"What do you mean?" Billy finally broke the awkward silence.

"Forget it," Whitey surrendered.

"Waitaminute. No. You cannot back out from us once you've started," said Billy. "What do you mean by stick straight up?"

"You know, uh, in your pants. Sometimes, mine's been doin' that."

"You got some kind of disease or something?" Billy innocently asked. "Mine ain't doin' that." Billy turned to Jimmy. "Does yours?"

Jimmy shook his head no. "But Skip warned me that could start happenin' on account of this whole puberty thing."

"Is it a bad thing?" Billy asked.

"I don't know," replied Whitey.

"Oh no, Whitey," Billy reacted. "I hope you ain't dyin' or nothing."

"He ain't dying you idiot," Jimmy clarified. "It is supposed to happen. At least, that's what Skip told me. It's called an erection."

"Does it hurt?" Billy asked Whitey.

Whitey's face turned red and then he chuckled and said, "No."

Suddenly, a distant voice said hello. It was Skip's. He stepped up onto the porch and took a seat beside Whitey. His blue eyes were brimming with hope and excitement as he announced he had news.

"Is it good news Skip?" Billy was anxious to find out.

"A bit." Skip answered.

Skip was making a quick stop by everyone's house to request a seven a.m. meeting down at the baseball diamond to discuss the game against the mob. "I promise to make sure y'all are home in time to leave for church."

4

Farmer Hayes's rooster, Sergeant, routinely announced the new day and awakened the restful Mississippi bayou neighborhood to the accompaniment of field sparrows and the distant high-pitched call of a loon. Jimmy stretched himself awake and felt the instant rush of blood surge from his toes to the roots of his brown hair. He called over to Billy: "wake up twin" and Billy forced his eyes to open and glanced at the alarm clock at his bedside. It was a quarter after six, far too early for Billy, and his grimace let Jimmy know it. Billy was not fond of early mornings.

Jimmy had already put on his trousers and was slipping on a plain, white T-shirt.

"Why you up?" Billy asked.

Billy had forgotten Skip's request to meet at the diamond before church. As he remained motionless in bed, staring up at his model planes, his eyes became heavy and in no time flat he was drifting back to sleep. Jimmy shook his head and walked over to Billy's bed and tore back the covers and tapped Billy on top of the head.

"Get up you knucklehead!" he ordered with a laugh.

Billy quickly snatched the covers back and tucked them around his body.

"Alrighty then, I'll leave without ya," said Jimmy.

Billy stretched himself long-ways and yawned. Suddenly, he remembered they had been thirteen for a full twenty-four hours and jumped out of bed. He hurried over to the closet, which was in the southwest corner of the room on the other side of the stairwell. Billy

34

opened the door and stood with his back against the height markings their father had carved in over the years.

"Measure me," he requested.

Jimmy agreed and walked over to the closet to check Billy's height. Billy was no taller than the tallest marking on the inside of the closet door. Jimmy asked Billy to measure him and he got the same result.

"Well, at least, we got something to pray for in church today," Jimmy said.

"Yeah," Billy agreed with a sigh. "Our growth spurt."

"Exactly," Jimmy then grabbed his Brooklyn Dodgers cap that was sitting on top of the dresser beside the west window.

Frustrated, they both headed downstairs to eat breakfast. When they were finished, they hurried off to meet up with Skip and the others.

T.J. was already at the baseball diamond when all the other boys arrived. Skip opened the floor by establishing that in order to win, they would have to commit to a more intensive practice schedule. Philly was the only one to complain about that. Skip warned his friends about Jonas's all-star batting average along with the team's reputation for cheating.

"What d'you mean?" T.J. had the least amount of experience with the mob.

"Well, I do know the few times we did play against them, whenever they had a runner on second, he'd read the catcher's signals and give signals of his own to their batter so he'd know what to expect," Whitey explained.

"Dat legal?"

"No," said Charlie, licking his fingers to slick back his perfect hair. "And I recall their catcher miscallin' balls for strikes and that one time Sampson was throwin' spitters, and them been outlawed since 1920."

"How come you's never called dem on it?"

"We did, but it did us no good except cause a huge fight," said Billy. "That's when my brother almost got punched by one of them. Ooh, I was ready to kill every last one of them mob boys."

"That ain't gonna happen this time," Skip interrupted. "Cause we're gonna keep this game squared up by havin' ourselves an umpire."

The boys agreed that having an adult there was the only way to ensure the game's integrity. Charlie suggested asking his uncle and dad to umpire. However, Skip disagreed. Whoever was elected would need to be impartial and free from any personal ties with the players. And, most challenging, he would have to be someone that the mob would agree on.

With the clock counting down the minutes until church, Jimmy and Billy knew they had better take the shortcut home through the woods. All the others, except T.J. who took the woods anyway, headed off through town. They were already dressed for church and had arranged with their folks to meet them there. Unfortunately, Jimmy and Billy had not thought that far ahead and needed to run home to get changed. The twins dreaded the shortcut through the woods, as a stretch of it passed by Slytown, which they had been told all their lives, was not a good place for white folk to wander. In the case of the twins, ignorance bred fear.

Jimmy and Billy followed T.J. deep into the verdant foliage. Shafts of sunlight cut through the treetops illuminating the green all around them. Their feet trampled a carpet of fallen leaves and twigs along the beaten path. Oak branches formed a colossal maze trimmed with grey Spanish moss that, on the lower limbs, hung clear down to the crest of the river of mist that hugged the ground.

For Jimmy and Billy these forests harbored a treasure of childhood lore. For as long as they could remember, they had been told stories about the Mississippi Delta bayou and the mysteries of its swamps. On those rare occasions when the boys weren't playing baseball, they would often go trekking into the forest to enjoy a cool dip in the swimming hole, or some frogging in the Big Black River.

As the trees multiplied, the boys' feet sank into the marshy floor and where the woodlands opened to the swamps, they would go their separate ways. T.J. would continue heading west to Slytown and the twins would cut south towards home.

"Shh! Stop for a minute. What's that sound?" Billy asked.

Jimmy and T.J. came to a halt and directed their ears towards the distance. There it came, the wailing of an ancient mellow rhythm from somewhere unknown.

"Dat be singun'," T.J. told them with a smile. "They must be baptizin already!"

"Where's it comin' from?" Billy asked anxiously.

"From over there, across de swamp. It's my cousin Ezekiel. He's ten and everyone just calls him Z."

T.J. pointed beyond the swamp as he began to descend the slope of uneven land.

"Come'on boys," he urged with a wave of his hand. "It's a beautiful sight!"

Billy and Jimmy's curiosities got the best of them, and they trudged through more forest until they came to another opening where a group of folks, dressed in white, were scattered about the bank of a clear and shallow pond. Standing knee-deep in the shallow and calm waters was a man wearing a white flowing choir robe and towering over a young boy similarly dressed. He gracefully placed his arm around the boy's waist and leaned him far back against the water. The water splashed as the boy's entire body was lowered backwards, submerged and then lifted out.

Jimmy grabbed his eager brother by the arm. "Hold up there," he hesitated. "I-I ain't too sure we should go there."

"Why not? T.J. said it was okay."

"I know but they're holdin' a sermon. I don't think they'd appreciate us intrudin'."

Billy paid no attention to Jimmy's last comment but broke away and caught up with T.J. Jimmy sighed and followed his brother. As they reached the other side of the pond, Jimmy and Billy looked around at the unfamiliar choir of faces praying and felt very much out of place. They watched, in silence, as two women stepped into the water and stood beside the pastor. Suddenly, they broke into song. Billy recognized the wailing yet joyful tune. It was the old Negro spiritual "Wade in the Water." One by one other voices joined, flowing into a low soulful mix of rhythmic vibratos. Eyes began to close and heads drifted. Some folks even raised their hands and rocked back and forth as if in a trance. As this continued, Billy turned to smile at Jimmy, who behind his look of discomfort appeared intrigued.

The pastor closed the song with a joyous prayer and then guided the boy to the riverbank. As the boy was returned to his mother, T.J. pointed her out as his aunt and the man beside her as his uncle. T.J. identified the couple standing with them as his parents. The pastor then made an announcement for everyone to "kindly return to da church for mo' sermon."

"Oh my gosh! Church!" Jimmy was reminded. "We best get!"

Jimmy yanked Billy, who was still in awe over the music, by the arm and together they dashed to the other side of the bank and down the trail. Layers of mud collected on the bottoms of their shoes and trails of sweat ran from their foreheads. Over and over, they reminded themselves of their tardiness and the trouble they were about to be in.

The path eventually dropped them off in Fist's back yard, where they cut into Green Valley Drive and dashed to their house. Being all a panic, the boys poured through the front door with their apologies. "Ahh crud!" Billy gasped. "My shoes are covered in mud."

Jimmy looked down to discover that his were too. They took off their shoes and brought them back outside. They went back in but walked no further than the foyer. The house was strangely silent. Jimmy instructed Billy to check upstairs while he checked the kitchen and the garage. They found no sign of anyone home. This was a nightmare come true and for a brief moment they just stared at one another, speechless.

"Well, what are we gonna do?!" Billy wanted to know.

"How am I supposed to know?"

"Well, I vote we pack up and leave town."

Jimmy disagreed. "I think it'd be best if we got cleaned up, put on our church clothes, and hurry down there."

"Are you kiddin'? Daddy's there!" Billy reminded him, appalled by his brother's suggestion. "He'll kill us the minute we walk through the door."

"But that's just it, he can't kill us!" Jimmy's surmised. "It's a church!"

"You're brilliant Jimmy! Plus, we'll be in the right place to pray for some help."

The boys hustled up to their bedroom and changed into clean slacks and white shirts. They felt ridiculous wearing ties, but put them on anyway. Then, it was down to the bathroom to douse their faces with water and run a wet comb through their hair to sleek out the tousled waves. In five minutes they were dashing out the front door.

5

❧✗❧

Family Fellowship Baptist was one of three churches; all Baptist, within Eugene's town limits. Inside, Tom sat like a boiling pot in the front row with his arms folded, legs crossed, and right foot shaking. Calmly seated at his side, with Jordan on her lap, was Ellen. She listened attentively while Pastor Cook stood up high on his white podium; his backdrop: a trio of tall, shelled windows framing a modest, hand-rubbed, oak cross as he read from Job Chapter 12.

Tom's thoughts couldn't help but stir over where the twins were and why they had disobeyed him. Last night they promised to return home in time for church. All of a sudden, Tom noticed that every head around him was bowed in prayer. Right away, he dropped his and folded his hands. As Pastor Cook smiled and reminded his congregation that patience was a virtue and the Lord wishes to see it in all his children, the back door creaked open and two thirteen-year-old boys tiptoed through. Their hearts were pounding and they were out of breath. The twins immediately spotted a conveniently empty pew in front of them and sat down without a sound. They ran their hands through their tousled brown hair and bowed their heads and pretended to join the prayer. Tom heard their entrance, but kept his head bowed. Although their defiance angered him, he was relieved to know that his sons were safe.

Jimmy and Billy searched the crowd for their parents. Amongst all the families, they saw their friends and some of the mob boys. They also saw the Widow Hayes with her sisters and Mrs. McCrosky was seated in the middle of it all, fanning herself with the week's bulletin. Up on the dais, with the rest of the small choir, was the top of Fist's head; he was staring into his lap to avoid being recognized. Billy was the first to spot Tom. Even from the back of the head, Tom looked furious. Billy elbowed Jimmy and unobtrusively pointed him out.

Because they didn't know what time it was, they had no idea how long the wait was going to be. And since neither had the guts to ask if anyone in their vicinity had a watch they stuffed their hands between their legs to stop them from fidgeting, and waited for the sermon to close.

"The offering tray!" Jimmy thought, "When they bring that out, we'll know how much time's left." But it seemed like another eternity passed before the ushers finally started circulating it. And when it reached the twins, they each dropped their head in shame. A donation would have been the least they could have done to compensate God for their tardiness.

Once the offering tray was collected, Pastor Cook asked for everyone to rise and join the choir in "Amazing Grace." The boys stood up, but their mouths remained shut. After the congregation had sung it one time through and then repeated the first verse, Pastor Cook gave the benediction. Although he was known for giving long, drawn-out closings, this one beat all because today it also featured a prayer, just as the boys' luck would have it. Finally, the pastor raised his hands high. He faced his palms out towards the congregation and invited everyone to "rejoice and follow our Lord's path, which he has so graciously set before us on this beautiful day."

As people rose from the pews and began filing out of the church, Jimmy and Billy were the first to exit. Once outside, they found the shade of a nearby giant, live oak tree and gazed up at the arched doorway of the small, quaint, white chapel and awaited their doom. Of course, the exuberant two-year-old Jordan, who was a sure to steal of every lady's attention, would cause the twins to expect some delay. As the small white church emptied itself, the boys saw the faces of everyone they knew except their parents. Soon, no more people were coming out and Jimmy and Billy began to wonder whether they might have missed their family.

Billy asked Jimmy if they should go back inside, but Jimmy thought it best to remain right where they were.

"Maybe Daddy's so mad, Pastor Cook won't let him come out till he promises God he ain't gonna kill us," Billy gathered.

It seemed like another eternity passed before Tom, Ellen, Rose and Jordan appeared in the church doorway. But the reason for the delay became obvious: Tom was absorbed in conversation with Farmer Hayes.

"I just wanna get home," Jimmy griped. "He's stallin' on purpose."

Jimmy was right; Tom was deliberately procrastinating. He knew if his boys were made to wait, that would prove the best form of punishment he could administer. Nearly ten minutes later, Tom shook hands with Mr. Hayes and walked over to the car with Jordan in his arms. Ellen and Rose followed close behind. Tom was 6'1" tall with an athletic build and broad shoulders. For being such a handsome man, he sure knew how to put on an intimidating face. He paid no attention to the twins as he opened the passenger door for Ellen and handed off Jordan. Even as Jimmy and Billy got inside the car, Tom did not acknowledge them.

The car ride home was dreadful. Not a word was spoken, not even between Tom and Ellen. The only sounds the twins heard were those coming from the car's engine and their pounding hearts. Once in the driveway, Tom asked if Rose would go and open the garage door. Now Jimmy and Billy were devastated. Opening the garage door had always been their job, never their sister's!

The boys followed their mother into the house. There, they were told to go change clothes and hurry down to the kitchen to help prepare that evening's meal. Although kitchen work was the boys' most hated chore, neither dared to argue.

Sunday supper was always the week's biggest meal, so the twins knew they were in for the long haul that afternoon. Chicken was invariably the main dish and it was prepared in one of only five ways. Today it was to be fried. Ever since they were eight, Jimmy and Billy were given the honor of plucking the dead chicken's feathers. But today, an even more stomach-wrenching task awaiting them: snapping the bird's neck, a task that Tom had previously always performed. The live chicken had been delivered the morning before and was being kept in a small pen out back. The twins made spectacles of themselves as the bird flailed and thrashed about. Billy threw up a little bit in his mouth, which made Jimmy want to do the same, but he stepped away to collect himself. The entire project consumed nearly two hours; including the fifteen minutes it took them to build up enough courage to actually kill the bird. When the chicken was finally bare the twins carried the naked bird to their mother and in return she handed each an apron and pointed to a heaping pile of fresh green beans. "I want all the ends snapped off," she instructed.

The boys nodded reluctantly and began working. Their hands still ached from gripping and pulling at all those feathers but their minds never once stopped thinking about their imminent punishment.

"Mama?" Jimmy said.

"Yes son," she answered patiently.

Jimmy paused a moment before he continued. "I'm sorry we was late to church. It was all my fault." This immediately sparked Billy's undivided attention. "I thought it'd be shorter goin' through the woods instead of through town, but I reckon I was wrong. Billy wanted to go with the other boys, but I kinda forced him to follow me."

"Jimmy?" Billy whispered into his brother's ear. "It was my fault we was late."

Ellen shifted her attention from the chicken to her sons. Jimmy and Billy looked so innocent in their aprons; how could she possibly be angry with her two babies who had grown so fast? With this thirteenth birthday, their entry to young adulthood had just begun and before long they'd be leaving for college and she'd lose them for good. Although Ellen wanted to take them both into her arms and keep them young forever, she knew her disposition must be firm. "What's taken with you two? Haven't your father and I told you enough times not to go through that part of the woods?"

"I know, but T.J. were with us, and nothin' bad happened," Billy said.

"T.J. was with us," she corrected him. "Now you boys know about them swamps bein' dangerous and just because T.J. was with you doesn't mean nothin' could go wrong. There might have been gaiters or rattlers in those woods. How's a body to know if one of you was bitten by something? Rules are rules."

"Yes ma'am," Jimmy answered.

"Billy?"

"Yes Mama. I'm sorry."

"Goodness knows you should be. Just be sure and tell your daddy that. You both are mighty lucky he's decided to spoil you another time and not take you's to the switch. Unless either one of you would prefer that?"

"No ma'am." They were quite sure.

"What do you think he'll do to us?" Billy wanted to know.

"In all honesty, I hope you both get the life-groundin' you deserve." Rose sneered as she entered the room to prepare the breading.

Ellen turned to face her daughter, giving Jimmy and Billy the opportunity to stick their tongues out at Rose.

"Rose, we don't need your opinion in this matter," Ellen said earnestly. "Now boys, when you're through with those green beans, there's more veggies to come."

Suddenly, there sang a voice from the front door. "Hello, dear."

"Rose, could you get the door for your Grama."

Grama Purdy was a trim and well-poised figure with a graying perm and tanned complexion. She was sixty years old. She marched into the kitchen with a 12-inch chocolate meringue pie in each hand and a happy, anticipatory expression on her face. Rose followed behind her carrying two quart bottles of homemade buttermilk. Ellen took both pies from her mother and placed them in the

Victorian highboy icebox. The two bottles of homemade buttermilk were placed in there as well.

"And how are my three beautiful grandchildren doin'? Come right over here and give your Grama some sugar," she said, holding her arms open for a big hug and kiss.

"Fine Grama," they answered.

"Ellen, I'll be right back. I'm just goin' out to the car to grab the peach cobbler."

"Rose, go on out to Grama and Grandpa's car and grab the cobbler, please and thank you!" Ellen instructed Rose.

The twins loved Grama's peach cobbler and chocolate cream pie with meringue topping. If it were up to them they'd just skip supper and go straight for dessert.

"Thank you Mama," Ellen gave her mother a hug. "And thank you for the buttermilk too!"

"Oh, you're welcome dear, it's my pleasure." Grama Purdy answered and walked over to the sink to wash her hands. "Land sakes! My goodness! What are you two boys workin' in here for? Here, let me take care of them veggies," she offered and went to grab the unfinished bowl. "Ellen, I plum forgot my apron at home, would you happen to have a spare?"

"No, no Mama, that's for the boys to do."

"Well then, let me take care of this here corn."

"That's for the boys as well."

"Now why on earth you got them doin' all this work? They should be outside playin' in the yard or something," she stated and began pulling back the husk from one of the ears. "Boys, why don't you go on outside? Go on now. Your grandpa's out there on the front porch talkin' to your daddy. But then it seemed to me that your daddy was really into readin' his paper, so your grandpa might need a bit of attention out there."

"Mama, please stop." Ellen took the corn from her mother and set it back down on the counter with the other ears. "Here Mama, let me pour you a nice glass of sweet tea."

"Ellen, did you hear about the new Winchester your daddy bought? I told him I didn't want another gun in the house, but he insists on keepin' it . . ." she continued on as she grabbed a turnip and began to chop.

"Mama!" Ellen spoke up.

"Yes dear, what is it?"

"The boys are bein' punished for comin' late to church. You were there. You don't recall them showin' up late to service?"

"Oh. That was them?" she realized and handed the knife back to Jimmy. "Well, God love the both of you. Now why in heaven's name were you boys late for Sunday service?"

"It was my fault Grama," Jimmy hurried to say.

"I'll explain it later," Ellen told her mother. "Boys, you have work to do and when you're finished with all that, I'd sure appreciate it if you'd both sweep up the dirt you traipsed on my foyer floor this morning."

Supper was ready around five o'clock and the boys were asked to set the dining room table. Everyone seemed to enjoy the meal except for Jimmy and Billy. For some reason, fried chicken didn't taste the same when you killed it yourself. After the meal, their duties continued with clearing the table and washing all the dishes. Everyone else retired to the front porch.

Jimmy washed and Billy dried. They were both very careful not to drop any of their mother's good dishes. The kitchen was hot from having the oven on all day. As Billy grew bored of wiping, he began humming to keep himself entertained.

"That sounds familiar," Jimmy said, while handing his brother another plate.

"What?" Billy stopped to ask.

"That tune you're hummin'."

"Oh, it's that song they was singin' down at the baptism. I liked it."

"I guess I weren't really payin' much attention."

"You know what?" Billy began. "I think I wanna learn me guitar."

"Don't you need a guitar first?" Jimmy remarked.

"Well yeah, but I can always ask for one this Christmas."

"Ain't those things kinda expensive?"

"Oh, it'd cost a pretty penny, no doubt. But it sure would be worth it."

"Why the sudden interest in guitars?"

"I dunno. But don't you think it'd be neat if I learned? Then me and you and the fellas could all sit out on the front porch together while I play. T.J.'s been playin' me some old 78's of guys like Robert Johnson and "Blind" Willie Johnson and all the new ones like John Lee Hooker and who's that one he told me about? Oh yeah. Muddy Waters. There's nothin' like that around here. Their music's so different. It's sad to think this but it's got so much more feelin' to it."

"Billy, since when do white folk play race music? You'd be in a whole mess of trouble. Plus, a fella just don't learn things like that overnight. I reckon it'd be forever before you even learn how to play even one song well enough to get through it."

"I could learn anything I put my mind to Jimmy. And it'd be worth it 'cause then I could learn how to write my own songs that maybe someday somebody else will wanna play."

"Maybe."

Billy didn't acknowledge his brother's lack of supportive enthusiasm. Instead, he tried to think of someway to change the subject. "Hey, Jimmy. Why'd you take all the blame for bein' late to church?"

Jimmy didn't respond right away. He wasn't exactly sure of his reasons; just that he felt like doing his twin brother a favor. "I reckon I kinda did it for the team, you know, to save it from losin' two players in case there's a groundin'."

"You think Daddy'll ground us?!"

"Maybe."

"So why didn't you just let me take the blame?"

"Cause Billy, you're the one with the best pitchin' arm."

"T.J.'s pretty good."

"True, but you're our star pitcher and better to be out a batter than a pitcher," Jimmy reasoned. "Well, this is the last of 'em." Jimmy finished washing the last dish and passed it to Billy. "What do we do now?"

"Maybe we oughta just go to bed."

"No, I think they'll let us come out on the porch with them; Grama and Grandpa are here. Besides it ain't like hidin' upstairs is gonna make Daddy forget about what we done."

"Okay, but I'd rather not stay long," Billy admitted and Jimmy agreed.

The boys quietly moved out to the front porch and found empty spots on the stairs. Grandpa was just about to embark upon another tale of "the Great War." Grandpa Purdy had been a pilot in the First Airborne during the First World War and became General of the 106th Airborne in the Second World War. Those years of experience provided him with so many almost unbelievable stories that were music to Billy's ears. Tom, on the other hand, did not appreciate his father-in-law's embellishments. It was uncommon for Tom to share stories of the war, but when he did, he spoke in a grave tone of the disastrous consequences of greed and ignorance.

Tom had served as an engineer with the 37th Engineer Battalion in the US Army and later the 209th Engineer Combat Battalion. From personal experience, he had seen how dropped bombs from German aircraft turned buildings and encampments of human life into dust. Also, he had experienced the menace of landmines, up close and personal. Too many good men had met an unfortunate fate after weeks of training and preparation from staying outside their detachment and tripping a hidden explosive wire. Tom had known men who had lost their lives within the first few seconds of battle and he also understood the psychological trauma that could result when a soldier held a dead friend in their arms knowing there was nothing they could have done to save him. But, when Grandpa Purdy talked, he bypassed these observations of war's horrors and went straight for the glory.

Jimmy and Billy sat with their mouths agape as Grandpa Purdy, once again, recounted the strife he had experienced from Fort Bragg to Normandy to Nottingham. Upon hearing his Grandpa's tales, Billy's imagination sent him inside the cockpit of a P-51D Mustang. He strapped himself in tight and pulled his goggles down over his eyes. The 1,490 hp Packard V-1650-7 Merlin liquid-cooled V-12 cylinder engine purred effortlessly as Billy called out all system checks to the radio tower. When Billy received clearance he led off down the short runway. As if his foot had done so a million times before, Billy tapped the brakes and the jet took off into flight. He continued to pull back on his controls and throttle up his airspeed until he reached 10,000 feet. He radioed out oxygen-check reminders to his wingmen before losing himself in the vast tangerine horizon up ahead. When he had his vision, Billy actually felt the true sensation of being in flight. It was a feeling of total happiness and absolute freedom.

Suddenly, there came a loud explosion from behind. The 37-foot wingspan of Billy's Mustang jerked out of place. Looking to the right he was blinded by the red-orange blaze of fire billowing from his right wingman's tail. Coming down at six o'clock, like a son of a bitch, Billy caught view of the bogie. It was a Me 262: a German aircraft with its 30-millimeter canon. As gravity and wind dispersed the exploded Mustang's smoldering remains, Billy's right wing came in square sight of the Me's gun. The enemy pilot was ready to open fire when Billy pitched down for a nosedive. He was earth-bound at such a steep degree that the compression of airflow over his aircraft's control surfaces was creating a risky situation. If Billy continued at this speed and pitch much longer his controls could freeze up rendering them useless for recovery from his dive. Upon reaching 1,000 feet and with the Me at twelve o'clock high, Billy reversed his pitch for a strenuous climb at full throttle. Like an angel, his Mustang rose, elevating no further than to level off his enemy from the rear. The Me 262 yawed left and right and Billy struggled to successfully secure his sight upon the target. It took a moment, but Billy remained focused and as soon as he locked in range on the Me 262, he pumped out a ray of cannon shells from his 0.5 inch Browning machine gun. Just then, a voice interrupted his reverie:

"Billy. Billy, honey it's time for bed," Ellen said softly.

Billy's blue eyes burst open to find two mosquitoes whining about his face. He swatted them away and noticed the sun had gone and everyone was staring at him. Jimmy, no longer at Billy's side, was standing in the doorway holding Jordan by the hand. Billy rose up and walked over to kiss his mother and grandparents goodnight. The boys put their little brother to bed, brushed their teeth, and went up to the attic.

The day seemed to have lasted forever and the boys were thoroughly drained. They stripped down to their briefs, put on their pin-stripped pajamas bottoms, and eased under their sheets. Moonlight shown soft through the east window and cast a bluish beam onto a strip of floorboards.

"Mind if I fetch the shades Jimmy?" Billy asked. "I don't want the sun wakin' me up tomorrow."

"Go ahead, but that dumb ol' rooster's gonna wake us up anyway," Jimmy reminded him.

"I can usually fall back asleep after Sergeant. It's the light that keeps me awake."

Billy hopped out of bed and hurried over to close the shades. Just as he slipped back under his covers there was a knock at their door. Both boys remained perfectly still. The knock repeated itself and the door opened.

Jimmy reached over and turned on his lamp and they both sat up. The sound of their father's approaching footsteps echoed loudly from the stairwell. The boys were once again reminded of the only reason why they disliked having a bedroom in the attic. Every time they were about to be disciplined, their father's long, drawn-out trip up the stairs felt like torture.

Tom came to a stop at the final step and looked at his sons with disappointment. He then went and stood before both beds. "What happened today boys?" he asked.

"Umm," Jimmy began. "We, um, took what I had thought would be a shortcut, through the woods, but we, um, we kinda found out it wasn't that short of a shortcut after all."

Tom wanted to laugh at his son's sorrowful response, but successfully contained himself. "All the other boys seemed to make it to church on time. I know I saw your friend Harold up with the choir. Why wasn't he late?"

"They had asked permission to meet their folks at church, instead of goin' home first."

Tom looked from Jimmy to Billy, to see if he had anything to say for himself.

"I guess we wasn't smart enough to think about doin' that," Billy admitted mournfully.

Again, Tom had to hold back his laughter. He said nothing in response except to deliver their punishment. At six o'clock in the morning, for the next few days, Jimmy and Billy would be spending the first few hours of their day helping Farmer Harlan Hayes with the chores around his farm.

Without saying "good night" or even "night" Tom left the boys to sleep.

Once Billy heard the attic door close, he spoke: "So I reckon this means no groundin'."

"I reckon not. He probably decided not to after the hell he put us through today, makin' us wait and all."

"Don't say hell like that Jimmy, it's still Sunday."

"Set the clock tonight, will ya? We can't afford to be late tomorrow."

"Yeah, and I might as well open them shades back up, seein's as we gotta be up before dawn anyhow."

Billy and Jimmy fell asleep to the symphony of crickets outside.

6

❧

Not a minute past six o'clock, Jimmy and Billy appeared at Farmer Hayes's barn door with a yawn and a "good mornin' sir!" Harlan Hayes was a medium-sized man of thirty-one years with a neatly trimmed beard and brown wavy hair. He thanked the twins for being so punctual and after clarifying that Jimmy's Brooklyn Dodgers cap was how to distinguish the two identical twins apart he led them around the barn and through the gate to the chicken coop. As he explained the basics of poultry farming, Farmer Hayes's pregnant wife Claudette appeared with two shallow bowls of what looked like cornmeal and thanked the boys for coming out. She handed over the chicken feed for the boys to distribute generously. The boys were sent to work. After feeding the chickens, they gathered up every egg from the hen house, remembering to keep the white eggs separate from the brown. After that, the boys were each handed a broom and told to clear all the cobwebs from around the outside of the barn. Next, they were instructed to check all the snake traps around the henhouse and reset any that may have accidentally been triggered.

Last, the garden had to be weeded. Billy moaned and groaned during the entire job and Jimmy ignored him hoping he would stop. When they were finished, Jimmy emptied their buckets full of weeds into Farmer Hayes's fire pit like he was instructed. He then carried the empty aluminum buckets into the barn to put them away.

The barn was fairly well lit with the mows on each end of the hayloft wide open, along with its front doors and the windows inside of the two horse stables. Jimmy admired the two Morgan horses. They were so beautiful he wished he and Billy each had one of their own to go riding together. Jimmy walked over to one of the stables and made a kissing sound and tried to establish eye contact with the animal. The horse looked at Jimmy for a moment but seemed to be distracted. Jimmy got an uneasy feeling in his gut and decided he better step away. The horse pounded his front hooves a number of times, which made Jimmy more nervous. Jimmy looked down at the horse's hooves but his eyes were immediately drawn to a sight that made his jaw hit the ground. Jimmy stepped backwards, tripping over his own feet, and fell to his ass.

"Billy!" Jimmy called.

Billy was on his way into the barn anyway to come looking for his brother. "What?"

Jimmy pointed at the horse. "What the hell is that?" Jimmy looked over at Billy to make sure Billy was looking in the right spot. "Do you see that? What is that?"

"Oh my," was all Billy could say at first.

There, before them, stood the horse with a giant erection.

"That's what Whitey was talkin' about Saturday night," Billy exclaimed with a crack in his voice.

"Oh my word!" they said together.

"Skip never explained it like this," Jimmy protested.

"Oh hell no! There is no way!" Billy's heart was beating a mile a minute.

Jimmy covered his face with his hands. He then pulled them away and looked at Billy and asked, "That's not even possible right? You know, for us."

"We best get outa here Jimmy before that horse finds a way out. If he gets loose and comes after us, he's liable to kill us with that thing!"

Jimmy couldn't agree more and off they ran to find Farmer Hayes so they could be dismissed. The time was now eleven o'clock in the morning. A grumbling noise in their stomachs inclined them to swing by home and grab a quick lunch before heading to the schoolyard. Ellen fixed them each a tuna salad sandwich. These were to be eaten slowly before leaving the house. Today was laundry day and Ellen did not need two stomachaches added to her already full schedule. The boys were still suffering from the shock of their mind-staggering experience at the barn, so they ate without saying a single word.

Meanwhile, down at the baseball diamond, the boys loafed about impatiently. They had already completed two rotations and were beginning to wonder just how late the twins were going to be. Skip had swung by the McGee house around nine o'clock and received the update from Mrs. McGee regarding the twins' punishment. The boys moaned and groaned about how nearly impossible it would be to maximize the rotation without its full complement that included Jimmy and Billy. Skip, on the other hand, saw a golden opportunity to truly put the boys' skills to test without the twins' assistance.

Skip encouraged the boys to continue with practice. He stepped into the batter's box and T.J. stepped up on the mound. T.J. went for the wind up and whistled a fast one that connected with the center of the bat. *Crack!* Skip hit a fly ball over Fist's head and into right center. Whitey was in the outfield and immediately went for the catch. He kept his head up high and his glove low to his chest. As the ball started to fall, Whitey stopped running and held out his glove. The catch was smooth.

"Yrrr-up Boston!" Skip announced. "Good job Whitey!"

Now it was Boston's turn at bat and Charlie rotated to the pitcher's mound. As soon as Boston found a comfortable stance, Charlie placed his right foot up to the edge of the rubber and mentally prepared himself for the delivery. As he swung his arms over his head, he spotted Jimmy and Billy running from around the front of the school. Charlie's attention left the wind-up and his arms dropped to his side.

"What're you doing? That's a balk you meathead!" Boston shouted to Charlie. "You can't be pulling that kinda stuff on game day. The ump will charge you with an error and put the mob's runner on first!"

"I know that," Charlie told Boston. "I stopped 'cause the twins are comin'."

"Oh yeah! Look!" Fist said with excitement and pointed straight ahead.

The boys all cheered and rushed to greet Jimmy and Billy, who had come onto the field. Skip could see that something else was on the twins' mind and pulled them aside to ask if everything was okay. Jimmy and Billy were not in the mood to discuss their horse encounter just yet, so they shook it off and told Skip they were both fine.

"Hey! You gettin' paid?" Philly wanted to know.

Skip rolled his eyes.

"Of course not you dummy," Billy mocked. "We're bein' punished."

Philly's expression tightened up from the insult and he was thinking of how to reclaim his dignity when Skip interrupted him.

"Hey y'all. I think I've figured out the perfect plan for connin' them mob boys into agreein' to an umpire."

All eyes and ears were focused on Skip as he slowly explained his proposal. He began by establishing that the game would require a total of four umpires, instead of just one behind home plate. The other three would all be in the field. Skip believed this was the only way to ensure equity and eliminate cheating. The umpire at home plate, of course, would call the balls, strikes and runs, and the others would determine the outs and safes at their designated bases. Additionally, if a ball landed near the foul line, only an official could determine whether or not it was in bounds. Skip suggested they ask Coach Fleming, the gym teacher, to be umpire-in-chief. He knew more about game rules than any other grown-up in town. This left three remaining umpires to be chosen, two of which the mob could select.

"Waitaminute," Boston abruptly interrupted. "You're gonna trust a bunch of natural born cheaters like them to pick two umpires?" The rest of the boys looked similarly concerned.

Before Boston could launch one of his rants, Skip raised his hands to signal that he still had the floor. He then proceeded to calmly but firmly explain that without giving the mob an equal say in the matter, they would never agree to these terms. Skip also said they should include a clause that prohibited relatives or anyone under the age of twenty to be chosen for this role. With this piece settled they could approach the mob and would do so on Saturday. Now they just needed to come up with one more field umpire and craft a plan to get the mob to agree to play peacefully with T.J.

Practice lasted until four-thirty and then everyone went home. With T.J. heading off in an opposite direction, it opened the floor for some private discussion around the concern of him playing. Skip had an idea. It was rooted from a particular encounter with the mob last summer. The boys would present the mob with a "contract" promising zero physical contact between any of them and T.J. At first, the boys were speechless. The idea seemed absurd.

"What about tag outs?" Whitey mentioned. This was a valid point that Skip hadn't considered.

"That actually shouldn't be a problem," said Charlie. "Because they'll all have gloves on while they're in the field, so they'll just be tagging him with their glove.

"Exactly," said Skip. "It ain't like it's skin-on-skin contact, so it should be fine."

Skip worked hard to sell the shrewdness of his plan and all the boys were seeing his point of view—everyone, that is, except for Jimmy who was still uneasy with allowing T.J. anywhere near the mob. It was not only T.J.'s safety that made Jimmy feel this way. He honestly believed that they were wasting their time figuring out ways to eliminate skin-on-skin contact because he was sure that the mob would not even agree to play baseball with a Negro.

"But that's just it . . ." Skip pleaded. "They'd be playin' against him not with him. It's a perfect argument to let T.J. play."

"No! It's a perfect way to get T.J. hurt or worse. I mean, why are you downplayin' that fact!"

"Are you tryin' to talk us out of playing this game, Jimmy?" Skip asked.

"I never said that. I agree we should definitely play this game against the mob, just not with T.J."

"Who else are we gonna get? T.J.'s too valuable of a player. He's our best infielder, he makes contact even on the toughest pitches and he's our fastest runner. Besides, there's no one else our age that plays. Jimmy, we gotta take this seriously. This ain't gonna be like how we've been playin' with our rotation and all. We need to be a real team with real strategies. T.J.'s quick on the bases. He'd be good at creatin' havoc for the mob and their pitcher 'cause they'd never know if T.J.'s gonna steal a base or not. And he'd be quick enough to get away with it."

"I know. But that ain't the kind of havoc I'm worried about, Skip. If them mob boys start runnin' their mouths and gettin' T.J. to feelin' bad about himself then he'll be miserable. And he won't have the confidence to be stealin' no bases or none of that."

"Like I said before, T.J.'s tougher than you think. And I'm sure after word gets around about this game there'll be plenty of adults there to make sure T.J. don't get hurt. The mob won't cause a scene if there's a bunch of adults there."

"Come on, Skip. You know just as well as I do that none of them grown-ups care a lick about a colored boy, except maybe all of our parents. If we let T.J. play, then we're not being good friends. He's not safe and that's all there is too it."

Skip disagreed and looked to Billy as if to say: please talk some sense into your brother! But Billy shrugged his shoulders in defeat. That's when Charlie spoke up in an effort to change Jimmy's mind. After Charlie spoke, Philly offered his rationale for T.J. playing. He believed that if T.J. were not included, it would actually send the wrong message because then they would be discriminating against him.

Jimmy couldn't help but recognize this as a valid point. Skip looked to Billy once more and Billy spoke up and encouraged his brother to agree with everyone else and allow T.J. to play. Jimmy's head was spinning. The warning signs around this issue were flashing an ugly red. He was certain that if he agreed to allow T.J. onto that field to play against the mob, T.J. would suffer unspeakable trauma. Still, there were no other ballplayers in their age group to fill T.J.'s position. As unfortunate as it seemed, including T.J. was their only option or else they may have to call the game off.

7

Once again, the practices on Tuesday and Wednesday morning made it only too evident that the team needed the twins if they were going to have any chance of winning. However, these practices also served to more clearly highlight to Skip each of the boys' talents and shortcomings. On Thursday morning, Jimmy and Billy made their final visit to Farmer Hayes. The sun was blistering hot and thick humidity smothered the wild green landscape along the sluggish bayou. The afternoon breeze showed up around two-thirty, but offered little relief and only swept up dust that stung the boys' faces.

"I can't stand this no more!" Philly exploded from center field. "It's just too damn hot. I feel like my sweat's about to boil."

Jimmy spun his head around and shot Philly a stern look. He knew if Philly kept it up, the others would join in and want to quit.

T.J. practiced his swing before settling into his stance. As Whitey wound up for the pitch, he could feel his muscles weaken. He followed through and delivered a quality pitch to T.J., who then knocked it high into center field. Philly saw the ball coming his way and took off running backwards with his glove high in the air.

"Turn around Philly!" Jimmy called to him. "He's gonna miss this one too!" Jimmy continued under his breath.

Philly paid no attention to the instruction and as the ball peaked, it crossed right into the sun's wicked glare and began a swift descent. Philly lost all sight of the ball. "Ahhh! I can't see anything!" he shouted, waving his arms back and forth above his head. A voice from the infield shouted: "Use your glove!" Philly took the advice and positioned his glove in front of the sun. At last, the ball came into view but it was too late for Philly to dodge out of the way before it whacked him in the head. "Ahhh!" he yelled out and fell to the ground.

"Ah'm sorry Philly, you all right?" T.J. asked as he rushed to his friend's side.

Philly lifted his head, wiped the sweat from his brow, and released a dramatic moan. As he looked up, he saw that everyone was standing around him with jaws gaping wide open. Philly had a huge red bruise across half of his forehead. "That's it!" Philly roared, throwing his mitt to the ground. "It's too dang hot out here. And now I got a headache. I quit."

"You can't just quit, Philly!" Jimmy protested. "You'll be fine."

"Yeah, let's stop," agreed Whitey. "I need some sweet tea or something."

"Y'all are a bunch of girls." Jimmy accused. He looked out at the collection of angry faces glaring back at him. "If you fellas wanna win this like y'all've been sayin' then . . ."

"Well I'm goin' home and sittin' in front of the fan," Fist interrupted.

"I'll come with." Charlie answered knowing that Fist's extremely attractive mother would be there. "Just let me go home first and get washed up."

Jimmy, Skip and T.J. chose to stay behind and work on their game while the others went home. After grabbing their piggy banks, Billy, Philly and Whitey returned to town for a soda at Russell's Drug Store located at the junction of Union and Front Street.

Tommy Lee Mason was busy cleaning the malt machine when Billy, Philly and Whitey all sat down at the long counter. Right away, the athletic and good-looking seventeen-year-old people magnet set down his damp rag and gave the boys his undivided attention and the three boys carefully inspected the modest list of treats handwritten on the chalkboard menu above on the long, oak back bar. They each decided that a root beer float sounded delicious, plus, it fell within their nickel-dime price range.

The boys asked Tommy Lee if he had heard about their game against the mob for control of the baseball diamond. It was news to him but in the middle of the boys explaining the general details Tommy Lee stopped and drew himself in to face the boys up close. He had a serious look on his face and he propped his elbows up on the counter and rested his chin on his hands in order to collect his thoughts.

"Waitaminute." Tommy Lee's tone was always collected and resolute. "Jonas and Felix were in here havin' a couple egg creams not even an hour ago and I overheard them goin' on about sendin' out some spy to come watch y'all play. That's strange though, I mean, if this game is so important I wonder why they were in here carryin' on and such and not out at their field practicin'. And why aren't y'all out doin' the same?"

"Cause it's too daggone hot out," stated Philly.

"Hold on, go back a second," Billy said. "What did you say about a spy?"

"Evidently, who ever they been sendin' knows an awful lot about baseball, you know, like technical stuff. And from what it sounds like, y'alls got some gaps in y'alls game. Maybe y'all oughta get some coachin'."

"What do you mean gaps?" Whitey asked.

Tommy Lee didn't know any specifics other than hearing that the boys were still using a rotation to practice. This was not an effective method of practicing for a real true-life baseball game.

Billy, Philly and Whitey all looked at one another and suddenly realized that they were thinking the same thing.

"Tommy Lee," Billy began with a smile, "how's about you givin' us some coachin'!"

Tommy Lee paused for moment. He was only needed at the drug store three half-days a week and the rest of his time was free. Taking these young talents under his wing might be fun, and most of all he really wanted to see them keep the diamond. Tommy Lee's eyes began to smile. "Billy, my boy, I think that's a fine idea!"

Billy, Whitey and Philly couldn't wait to inform the others. For the first time in their lives they considered abandoning their root beer floats just so they could hurry back to the diamond and tell Skip, Jimmy and T.J.

Tommy Lee overheard them mention T.J. and was quick to step in. "You boys aren't seriously including T.J. in this game are you's?"

At first, the three boys were a bit jarred by Tommy Lee's tone. If anyone in town had always supported their friendship with T.J. it was Tommy Lee Mason.

"I've always meant to ask y'all," Tommy Lee began. "Are y'alls parents alright with y'alls playin' with him? I mean it ain't exactly the norm, you know."

"What are you sayin?" Whitey asked defensively.

Tommy Lee realized his intentions were being misread and he switched up his tone and apologized. "I'm just worried about T.J.'s safety. Isn't there someone else in Skip's class that can help y'all out? Think about it, them mob boys are gonna tear T.J. apart not to mention y'all don't think that everyone in town's not gonna be there to watch y'alls game? Lord knows what half the folks around here will have to say about him bein' there. I know he's real good and all but I think it's a bad idea. I think y'all need to find a replacement."

"No way!" the three boys practically spoke in unison.

Billy continued: "We've done discussed this issue already. And my brother had the same opinion that you do. He probably still does. But we all finally agreed that ain't nobody gonna replace T.J. He's our friend. Folks around here are just gonna have to settle down and accept it."

Tommy Lee smiled at Billy with a twinkle in his eye. He admired Billy's passionate conviction "I can't say that I disagree with you there. Maybe you boys are onto something. Maybe seein' T.J. there is just what folks in this here town need." Tommy Lee paused for a moment and let out a sigh. "I just can't help but worry for his safety."

8

At half past ten the following morning, Tommy Lee rounded the boys up at home plate to discuss a game plan. He would first need to watch them play a few rounds in their current rotation to evaluate whose skills best fit into which position. But already there was a setback: Whitey was not present. As usual, Skip and the twins had stopped by Whitey's house that morning to pick him up but found themselves interrupting a serious family discussion and Whitey was unable to leave. This meant Tommy Lee would not immediately get the entire picture.

Tommy Lee was able to staff the team's starting pitcher position before they even began to play. Billy McGee had the fastest fastball, the most intimidating curve, and the lowest drop and was the most consistent for throwing strikes. However, to plan for the eventuality that Billy's right arm may grow tired, Tommy Lee insisted on selecting a relief pitcher. Billy was appalled and tried arguing the case for his invincibility, but Tommy Lee insisted on staging T.J. as his relief. At first, warning signals were blaring in Tommy Lee's head but he was able to work through the discomfort realizing that T.J. was the strongest candidate for this role. Skip, however, could not quiet his concerns and was determined to have a word with Tommy Lee as soon as an appropriate opportunity arrived. Surely, all chaos would explode within the mob if a black boy stepped up to the pitcher's mound.

Remaining at home plate as batter, Tommy Lee instructed the boys to rotate among the infield and outfield positions. Billy pitched to Tommy Lee who hit the ball out to various areas of the baseball field. Tommy Lee kept the boys rotating until potential for a specific position caught his eye. He would then ask that player to remain and continue working that particular position until further notice. The main glitch with this method, however, was that second and third base never had a runner, so Tommy Lee had to judge each boy's ability to render a putout solely based on his performance at first base.

One of Tommy Lee's early hits was a line drive up the middle fast past Billy's head. Somehow, T.J. managed to bolt in front of it and steal the catch. Tommy Lee was highly impressed and T.J. remained as shortstop.

Charlie and Boston also demonstrated a knack for defending the infield. Charlie stopped a couple of grounders from hopping by and they both exhibited swift and accurate reaction throws. The longer Tommy Lee watched, the more comfortable he felt with placing Boston at first base and Charlie at second.

Fist and Philly, however, were the team's weakest links. Fist couldn't catch a fly ball if his life depended on it and he wasn't much of a runner. But while he did have good aim and a relatively decent throwing arm, Tommy Lee was uncertain about where he should go.

Even more of a concern was Phillip Tupper. His weight slowed him down so infield was out of the question. It might not take as much work getting Philly up to par on fly ball saves, but Tommy Lee just was not comfortable relying on him in such a valuable position as outfield. Suddenly, it dawned on Tommy Lee that Philly's stocky build was perfect for catcher. Tommy Lee had Jimmy bat for a while so he could watch Philly in action behind home plate. It wasn't long before everyone could see that Philly had the necessary skills. All Philly would need to do is work on his throwing and memorize the signals.

Skip and Jimmy exhibited fortes in both the infield and outfield. However, the more Tommy Lee watched everyone interact, the more it became clear that these two would be more valuable as outfielders. And according to the boys, Whitey's skills could shine best in the outfield as well. Now came the task of determining their specific locations. Though the mob only had two left-handed hitters, one of them was their star hitter: Jonas. That meant that it was most probable that home run balls would be hit into either center or right field. Tommy Lee figured that if Whitey took center field, then Skip and Jimmy could be ready on either side of him in case of a biff. The result of this decision was that Fist would assume the team's last remaining unassigned position of third baseman.

With that out of the way, Tommy Lee could begin grooming the boys for strategy and synergy. It was going to take some hard work for these boys to become a fully capacitated team that didn't rely alone on Jimmy's batting, Billy's pitching and T.J.'s speed and agile fielding. To assist, Tommy Lee planned to recruit his friends to simulate an opposing team. The boys needed experience with tagging out runners, attempting double plays, and preventing stolen bases. Equally important, the boys needed to strategize their offensive tactics and Tommy Lee would have to evaluate everyone's at bats to draft the team's official batting order. All in all, there was a lot of work to be done in less than two weeks.

As the hot afternoon lingered on, there was still no sign of Whitey. With every ball that Tommy Lee hit to the boys, he offered a dozen or so suggestions to correct their hang-ups. To train Philly, Tommy Lee intentionally popped up a few balls straight in the air. Philly missed them all and every time used the same excuse that he couldn't see where the ball was going.

"Well, of course you couldn't," Tommy Lee told him. "You gotta take off your mask. You're almost never gonna see to catch the ball with that mask on."

The next ball Billy delivered was knocked high above the plate and Philly stood up to catch it. He tore off his mask and dropped it behind him. As the ball descended, Philly stepped backwards and tripped right over his mask. Both he and the ball fell to the ground with a resounding thump.

"Damn it!" he exclaimed.

"Philly. Never let that mask outa your hand. When you're needin' to catch a pop fly, take the mask off, but hold onto it. And hold it away from you, don't ever drop it. If you accidentally do let go of it, make sure you kick it out of your way, away from the direction you're headin'. Oh! And another thing, if the ball pops out of your glove after a delivery, always take off your mask."

Philly nodded and returned the mask to his face and positioned himself for the next play. Just then, Whitey came running into the schoolyard. He was drenched in sweat and out of breath. As soon as he entered the diamond, he collapsed to his knees. The boys surrounded him in a tight circle, anxious to hear his news.

Whitey knew the boys were not going to be happy about his news, so he made sure to explain it in a straightforward way. Sure enough, his words struck like thunder.

"When?" the back of Billy's voice trembled.

Whitey paused a moment. He was so afraid to answer but knew he had no other choice. He drew in the longest, deepest breath of his life before faintly uttering: "Tomorrow."

A dismal hush settled over the circle of friends. This was not possible, they each thought to themselves. It wasn't like Whitey was moving to the next town or somewhere nearby. He was leaving the South altogether. What's more, he would miss the most important baseball game of their lives! Whitey's tongue spilled over with apologies. He wished with all his heart he could reverse his father's decision to take the job in Pittsburgh. Whitey searched for someone to respond. He felt so alone and needed any form of reassurance. This was truly a milestone and a tragedy.

"Um," Fist spoke up. "Where exactly is Pittsburgh anyway?"

"It's in Pennsylvania, stupid," Boston said derisively. "You know, the Pirates. Forbes Field. Baseball! Hello!"

"Oh, yeah. I figured that was a stupid question."

"Hey Whitey," said Skip. "Your folks must have known about this? I mean folks just don't make decisions to move up north overnight. It's dangerous up there—no offense Boston."

Boston rolled his eyes.

Whitey nodded and explained that his parents had known for some time but for some reason, which they didn't share with him, waited till the last minute to tell him.

The boys realized they had hit a dead end. Perhaps this was God's way of keeping T.J. safe since they were obviously going to have to call off the game. There was no way of finding a replacement for Whitey.

After a long period of heavy silence, Charlie had an idea. "I think I got an idea! Y'all remember that boy that came over with the mob last Saturday?"

Everyone but T.J. and Tommy Lee knew of whom Charlie was referring.

"What about him?"

"How's that going to work? He runs around with the mob. And, besides, all he does is fetch their balls for them. There's probably a good reason for that. Like he don't know how to play or ain't any good," Philly insinuated.

Skip agreed that it was a far fetch but at this point, what other options did they have? "Good idea Charlie. I mean, we're goin' there tomorrow anyway to give them boys our proposal, so we might as well ask the boy. It's at least worth a shot, right?"

"You fellas goin' there tomorrow?" asked T.J.

"Yeah, remember? I told you last night we decided that. We have that proposal for them about the umpires," Skip reminded him.

"Hold on. How we ever even gonna get the mob to agree to this boy comin' with us in the first place," Jimmy pointed out. "They'll never agree to that."

Boston agreed and started in with his mile-a-minute two-cents until out of nowhere, Skip ad-libbed, "We, um, we'll kidnap him."

Skip could hardly believe his own words and based on the reaction from everyone else, the idea seemed preposterous.

Skip scrambled to formulate an explanation. "I mean, obviously we can't force him to come. But I reckon the mob ain't makin' it worth him stickin' around."

"Well obviously they do. He's stuck around so far," Jimmy pointed out.

"Yeah but he probably don't know anyone else. He's obviously new in town. I mean, I ain't ever seen him before. So, all we gotta do is somehow grab his attention to get him alone long enough to ask him. After that it's up to him. He's either gonna wanna switch or he's happy bein' with them."

"That makes sense," said Charlie. "I can't imagine he likes hanging out with the mob. They're nothing but trouble. Him being new and all, he probably doesn't know anyone else to run around with. So he's probably feels stuck with them."

"Okay, so how you figure we're gonna talk to him without the mob knowin'?" Philly questioned. "And let's say he does switch to our team. They're gonna know right away and they're gonna come lookin' for him."

"So let them come lookin'. Who cares, they don't own the boy. If he chooses us, then there ain't nothing more to say about it. Here's what we're gonna do." Skip continued to improvise. "Since me, Jimmy and Billy are the ones goin' to talk to the mob, the rest of you all need to stay far enough behind where the mob can't see you or hear you or nothing. They cannot know you're talkin' to this boy or they'll definitely interfere. Now, after I convince the mob to agree to our plan, we gotta figure out somehow to separate that boy from the rest of them so's y'alls can be alone with him to talk to him and hopefully get him to switch. Hmm." Skip began to pace a few steps back and forth. "I got it! We're gonna sweeten the pot by convincing them to give us one turn at bat against their pitcher if we give them a turn to bat off our star pitcher Billy. Hopefully, they'll go for it, and we'll have Jimmy hit because he's got the best chance of sending the ball where we need their ball-retriever to go."

"Where's that?" Fist asked.

"Out to wherever we're hidin' you ding-bat," Philly ridiculed. "Dang!"

Fist scowled at Philly but Philly didn't pay him any attention.

"Exactly," confirmed Skip. "That's how we'll get him alone with you. Make sense?"

"There's that long fence there. We can hide behind it," suggested Charlie.

"But how y'all gonna keep the mob from realizin' their ball retriever ain't comin' back with their ball?" Tommy Lee pointed out. "And what's your back-up plan if Jimmy's aim ain't so great?"

"Simple. We'll bring an extra baseball with us and just hand them that ball as a replacement offering and pray to God they don't refuse." There was a dismal cloud of doubt glaring down over Skip's suggestion. Skip swallowed the lump in his throat. He looked at Jimmy with serious eyes and stretched his arm around Jimmy's shoulders. "We'll all be prayin' for you Jimmy McGee. This is all pretty much gonna rest on your batting skills. But I got a hundred percent faith that your aim's gonna be just perfect."

Although the idea and all its intricacies seemed rickety, the boys were desperate at this point. If only there were more boys their age in town.

"Well, let's just go with this for now and if tonight any of you come up with a better idea, then I'm all ears."

Skip went on to explain his proposal for umpires. Pastor Cook, who sometimes umpired for the adult men's church league on Friday nights, had always advocated mixing Negros with whites on the ball field so his presence would provide additional protection for T.J. Although in most quarters, Eugene was habitually prejudice, however, there was a tiny slice of progressiveness just yearning to break free the rest of its primitive population.

9

Jimmy and Billy walked side-by-side behind Skip up Locust Street. The rest of the boys trailed a block or so behind. The mob was busy running plays and as soon as they spotted Skip and the twins, they abandoned their positions and assembled as one apocalyptic force on the pitcher's mound.

"I count ten of them," Jimmy whispered to Billy and Skip.

"So? Shouldn't there?" asked Billy.

"I was hopin' one would be missin' so's we'd know whose been spyin' on us."

"Ahh! Smart thinkin' Jimmy," Skip commended.

Billy nodded in agreement.

Skip walked fast and confident and stopped short of Jonas whose nostrils flared open. The two boys exchanged nods and cross-fired intimidating glares. Skip opened the floor.

Meanwhile, the rest of the boys had gathered behind a tall, brown clapboard fence. They were too far away to hear the conversation and had to take turns peeking through a single knothole in the fence.

Across the street, an unknown innocent-looking couple was busy doing their yard work. Off and on, they glanced suspiciously at the boys. Charlie was getting nervous that the couple might blow their cover.

"I'm goin' over to talk to them," said Charlie. "Philly, you want to come with me?"

"I'll come!" offered Fist.

"No!" Charlie objected.

"Why not?" Fist about blew his top and their cover.

"Shh!" Charlie hushed him.

Philly agreed to join Charlie and the two boys dashed across the street to explain their situation to the elderly couple. Within a few minutes, they rejoined the boys, behind the fence and Charlie took the next turn at the knothole.

"I wish I could read lips," said Charlie. "It's not lookin' good right now."

"I wanna see," Boston insisted and forced Charlie aside.

Boston could see that Skip was the only one doing any talking. After less than half a minute, he stepped away, shaking his head. "This is too stressful, I can't watch."

"You need to calm down boy," Charlie scolded, still annoyed that Boston had pushed him out of the way.

Now, Whitey was at the knothole and urging everyone to be quiet. "They're breakin' up. Jonas just handed Billy the ball. Billy's gonna pitch first."

"Good, just like Skip planned," said Charlie.

Billy took the mound and warmed up to pitch to Rusty, the mob's first baseman.

Billy remembered Tommy Lee's' advice not to deliver anything special to the mob. They did not need to receive any further insight into Billy's faculty than what they already understood.

Rusty swung late at the first delivery and it landed right in for the first strike. The second pitch was a swing and fouled back out of play. On the third pitch, Rusty hit a rocket for a base hit to first. The mob cheered him on as Rusty landed safely on the bag.

Now it was Jimmy's turn at bat and Sampson, the mob's pitcher, took the mound. He had such an arrogant expression on his face and Jimmy was equally sure of himself as he panned his eyes across the shoddy outfield. He knew his hit had to be just a few yards left of center and far enough to either hit the grass and bounce into the street or clear the outfield altogether.

All of a sudden, Skip called time and hurried over to whisper into Jimmy's ear.

"Do not hit a homer. Remember?" Skip warned him. "You got that look in your eye Jimmy."

"I know, I know," Jimmy sighed.

Jimmy knew that a home run today would only compel the mob to intentionally walk him during the real game. Skip stepped away and Jimmy took a few practice swings before he settled into his stance. Sampson wound up for the first pitch and Jimmy swung for a fly ball loft to the left.

On the second pitch, Jimmy connected better and the ball darted low over Sampson's head and hit the ground hard with enough momentum to bounce twice and roll into the street and behind the fence.

"Perfect!" Jimmy, Billy and Skip all thought to themselves.

Without even being instructed, "Slave" took off after the ball. Skip reached into his pants pocket and gripped the extra ball. So far, everything was proceeding just as planned.

As Slave stepped into the street and reached down to pick up the baseball, a whispered voice called out to him. Panicked, the boy froze still. He wanted to look up but couldn't.

There was an awkward silence until Boston broke it with: "Why ain't he lookin' at us?"

"Cut it out Boston!" Charlie snapped. He then softened his tone to speak to Slave. "Sorry kid but my friend here sometimes can't help himself on account of him being a Yankee." Charlie explained to Slave.

"What? I just wanted to know," Boston said, throwing up his hands.

Charlie's voice sounded familiar to the boy. He held his breath and looked up in the direction of the voices. There, just a few feet away, hiding behind the tall, wood fence stood five eager boys. Slave peered out beneath the brim of his red cap. His light brown eyes did not recognize a single one of them. For a moment, he just stood there, holding the ball in his half-open, left palm, wondering: if he ran would they chase him down? Uncertain, his head dropped back down to the ground.

Charlie stepped forward and assured the boy that he and his friends meant him no harm. After hesitating for a moment, the boy lifted his head again and made eye contact with Charlie. The boy had a soft, olive-toned complexion. His voice was small and high-pitched and for being as tall as Charlie, he had a frail frame for his shoulders swooped as low as his self-esteem. His real name was Sam and curiously enough it didn't take long for Charlie to convince him to leave the mob and join their team.

Meanwhile, Jonas and the mob had noticed the disappearance of their ball-retriever. Skip caught on as the mob was looking around so he motioned to the twins that it was now time to leave. As planned, Skip pulled a spare ball from his pants pocket and handed it over to Jonas. Jonas looked confused.

"What the hell's that for?" Jonas wanted to know. "Slave will get our ball. You go ahead and keep yours."

"This here ball's band new. Why wouldn't you want it? We can go grab your ball on our way out. It'll be easier."

Jonas poked his head up over Skip's shoulder and looked out beyond the outfield.

"No. We'll wait for ours. It'll come back," Jonas insisted.

"All right. Suit yourself," Skip replied. "Asshole!"

Jimmy and Billy were caught off guard by Skip's remark. It was clearly an attempt to pick a fight, which was exactly Skip's intent, to stall for additional time.

"What'd you just call me?"

"I called you an asshole," Skip replied clear as day. "What? Could you not understand me the first time?"

Billy was enjoying this but Jimmy was preparing to run for cover as Jonas came forward and stood glare to glare with Skip.

"Let's you and I go! Right now!" Jonas insisted.

Without a second to spare, Jimmy intercepted. "That's enough you two," he said and pulled back on Skip's left shoulder. "Let's just get their ball back to them and go."

Skip backed away but Jonas was not about to let down.

"Come on Jonas," Sampson spoke up. "There's people outside. You're gonna get us in trouble again."

"Who cares," Jonas stated. "We only got a week left in this stinkin' lot anyhow."

"That's right," one of the boys from the mob agreed. "Cause pretty soon y'alls diamond's gonna be ours."

"Oh no it ain't," said Billy.

Jimmy was about to forcibly direct his brother and Skip to their exit when all of a sudden, the mob's baseball came rolling up on the ground behind them. It stopped short of Skip's heels. Skip looked behind him to see what it was and could not believe his eyes. "Why don't those boys listen to anything I say," he thought to himself in frustration.

Now Jonas was fully charged with suspicion and began to make his way into the outfield. Skip and the twins followed behind him trying to think of someway to inconspicuously warn the others of Jonas's approach. At the outer rim of center field, Jonas stopped and looked ahead at the brown clapboard fence.

By now, Charlie and the others had abandoned their hiding place and were desperately looking around for where to go next.

"Look," Philly pointed to the elderly man who was motioning for them all to come into his garage. The boys obeyed but Slave thought it was best to stay behind as they hurried off. The garage was small and dark inside and so it was easy for the boys to not be seen. Moments later, Jonas stepped into the street and spotted Slave.

"Get back here," he snapped. "Right now!"

Slave hurried over to join Jonas who then gave Skip and the twins a sneering goodbye before returning to the lot.

Skip and the twins looked around and, to their relief, their friends were nowhere in sight.

"Well, what are we gonna do now Skip?" Jimmy asked.

"We're in a heap of trouble," stated Billy. "We'll never find a replacement for Whitey in time."

"Hey look," Jimmy said, pointing to Charlie and the others who were now exiting the garage and thanking the elderly man for his assistance.

"Let's just grab them and get off this street," Skip insisted. Once they were all clear of Locust Street, Skip stopped and turned around to ask: "Who threw the ball?"

Awkwardly, no one answered.

"Hello? Is not one of you's answering 'cause you're all guilty?"

Finally, Fist admitted: "Um, I did."

"Of course you did," Skip said under his breath. "Why would you throw the ball Fist? Why would you do that?"

"He did it for you," said Boston. "One of us had to or Jonas was gonna clobber you."

"I had the whole thing under control," Skip insisted and then turned to get confirmation from the twins, "Didn't I?"

Jimmy and Billy felt trapped so, with nowhere else to go, they conformed to answering "yes."

"We only have a week left until this game fellas and now what are we gonna do? Any of you's got any bright ideas?"

"Let's go back to the diamond and we can talk about it there," Jimmy proposed and everyone agreed.

The walk back seemed to take forever. Skip's thoughts were going a hundred miles per minute and he was in no mood to talk.

The sun was blistering from high above. There appeared to be a rhythm to the waves of heat that moved across the road in the distance ahead. The boys were beginning to feel hungry and Philly offered his house for lunch but Skip wanted them to first swing by the baseball diamond and check for T.J. By the time they got there, Skip had calmed down and apologized to Fist for being so quick-tempered. T.J. was there, waiting, so the boys filled him in on their unproductive encounter with the mob.

"Well, I reckon we should go grab lunch now so no more of today gets wasted," said Jimmy.

"I just ate, so I'm just gonna hang 'round here," said T.J.

"You don't have to be nervous T.J.," Philly assured him. "You're always welcome at my house."

T.J. smiled but said he'd rather head into the woods and find a nice tree to climb and relax.

The boys left for Philly's house and ate as quickly as they could. Mrs. Tupper asked why they were all so quiet and they filled her in on their news and asked if she had any suggestions. The only ideas she could offer involved asking one of the older boys to play, but Skip explained how that went against the terms their team had agreed upon with the mob.

It all seemed hopeless. If only there was a way to keep Whitey around for a few more days. But Whitey assured them that his father had already made it clear that delaying the move was not an option.

"We should all pray tonight," Billy said. "Real hard-like."

"Yeah, for a miracle," said Boston.

The boys somberly made their way back into town and when they approached the baseball diamond T.J. was there, talking to someone else.

"Who's that?" Billy asked.

"Holy Moses," Charlie blurted out. "It's that kid. The one we just tried to kidnap. Slave. I-I mean Sam."

It took walking a few more steps closer before the boys realized that Charlie was right. As they stepped into the diamond, Sam turned around to see the boys and immediately clammed up. Skip tuned into the boy's anxiety, so he approached him with a soft voice and a smile to assure him that he was in a safe place.

"How'd you get here?" Charlie asked Sam.

"He walked you idiot," Boston declared.

"I know that, I meant how did he get here without them other boys knowin'?"

It took a moment for Sam to speak, but when he did, he explained that he was tired of being treated like "scum" and finally stood up for himself and left.

"How'd you wind up with them boys anyhow?" Billy wanted to know.

"My mom and I live on Locust Street. We just moved here from Jackson. I saw them boys playin' and . . . and I don't know nobody else in town."

"Why'd it take you till now to leave them?" Philly couldn't resist asking

Sam shrugged his shoulders. "I guess 'cause y'alls are the first other kids around town that I've met."

"What's your last name?" Skip inquired.

"It's Russo," T.J. informed them all.

"Ah! You're Italian!" Boston identified. "Me too! You and I are gonna be good friends. I can already tell."

"Just 'cause he's Italian? What? You' are gonna ride off into the sunset together," Billy mocked.

Boston walked over and put his arm around Sam. "Yep! We're gonna be best buds. It make it even better if he was a Yankee!"

"So Sam, tell me something." It was obvious that Skip had something deep on his mind. "How come them boys weren't lettin' you play baseball?"

"Yeah!" Philly chimed in. "And why you lettin' them call you Slave?" Philly then turned to T.J. and apologized for the terminology.

All of a sudden, Sam clammed up again. "So much for bein' best buds," he thought to himself. He wanted so bad to be accepted by these boys. He needed a nice group of friends but what he was about to admit could be a definite deal-breaker.

"Uh, I um, I don't play."

"Never?" Skip found this hard to believe.

With utter embarrassment, Sam shook his head no. "I ain't never even swung a bat before."

The boys all just stood there, completely speechless.

Then, Skip asked: "Well you've thrown a ball before? Right?"

Sam's head dropped to the ground after he shook it "no."

With this, the boys all broke out into a symphony of theatrical moans and groans. Sam became desperate for a way to prove some competence. He did not want to return to Locust Street. "I can run fast . . ." he muttered and then wished he had kept that piece of information to himself as the boys all began to laugh hysterically.

Suddenly, Sam felt a gentle hand below his chin. It was Skip's hand.

"Look up at me," Skip asked.

Sam slowly raised his head to learn that Skip was not reacting along with all of the others.

"Don't listen to them," he assured Sam. "They'll get over it."

Skip smiled and Sam half-smiled back. "So, um, do you understand the game? You know, the rules and all? I mean you must have learned something while you was watchin' them boys. And all them times you had to fetch the ball you never once threw it back?"

"Oh yeah, I always did."

"So you can throw a baseball?"

Sam just shrugged his shoulders.

Skip ordered all of his friends to quiet down. Although he couldn't help but think that giving Sam a chance would be a huge mistake, Skip knew they were out of options. He looked the boy twice over. Although Sam appeared scrawny, he did have long forearms. That was a start, Skip thought to himself.

Just as Jimmy and Billy went to tell Skip that he'd be crazy to give this boy any further consideration, Tommy Lee appeared from behind. "Hi there, my name's Tommy Lee," he greeted enthusiastically, with a smile and threw out a welcoming hand.

It took Sam a moment to realize what he should do before extending his own. As the two shook, Tommy Lee's face was overcome with a look of curiosity. There was something oddly familiar about the boy. Tommy Lee tilted his head and opened his mouth as if to communicate a thought. Sam's eyes grew wide. He was smart enough to understand that Tommy Lee's opinion could make or break his security on the team. The terrified look on Sam's face remained for a few moments until Tommy Lee's expression relaxed and he gave Sam a warm smile. Sam was relieved and smiled back.

"Uh, Tommy Lee," said Billy. "I think there's something real important you oughta know."

Tommy Lee turned to acknowledge Billy. "Oh yeah, what's that?"

"This boy here ain't never actually played any baseball before."

"Oh," Tommy Lee said plainly. "Well, then," he paused for a brief moment. "I reckon we got ourselves some work to do."

Every jaw, except for Skip's, dropped.

Tommy Lee turned to Skip and inquired about the mob agreeing to all terms of the proposal, to which Skip smiled and nodded with a composed yes.

With a new member on board, Tommy Lee explained that he would be requiring twice as much effort and dedication from each and every team member. Tommy Lee's tone was authoritative and his words fast, giving no opening for interruptions. He knew if anyone did squeeze in an opinion; its resonant disrespect towards Sam might exterminate all hope of instilling some confidence in him. When Tommy Lee was finished, he clapped his hands together twice and told everyone to take their positions.

Tommy Lee escorted Sam out to center field with his right arm around the boy's shoulder. Tommy Lee briefed the rookie on an outfielder's responsibilities. The other boys didn't budge, but stood there staring vacantly (and a bit incredulously) at the back of Tommy Lee's head. Tommy Lee had sounded as though training this newbie was going to be some sort of picnic. There was no way this boy was going to acquire enough skill in the little time they had. They were guaranteed to lose the diamond now. But as fate would have it, with Whitey gone, there was no other available boy in town their age. The other boys in Skip's class were all cousins and out of town, with family, that weekend and, other than the mob; everyone else their age was a girl. And girls don't play baseball.

As soon as Tommy Lee was finished with Sam, he hustled back to home plate and sent Whitey out to center field to assist. Whitey was reluctant to help Sam but not about to argue with Tommy Lee. The first pitch Billy delivered, Tommy Lee knocked high into center field. Sam did as instructed by Whitey and watched the ball carefully. He promised to punish himself hard if he screwed up this first catch. Although the sun was casting a nasty glare along the ball's path, Sam watched. He lifted Whitey's glove high into the air and waited for the ball to go in. A noise (*thunk*!) came from behind, but Sam ignored it. After waiting some more, Sam wondered if maybe he had already caught the ball. He had been holding up that glove for a long time now and couldn't understand why he hadn't felt anything go in. Sam reached up with his right hand and felt around inside of the mitt. It was empty. Suddenly, his misfortune became all too clear. The sound he had heard behind him was the ball hitting the ground. Sam turned around and sure enough, lying deep in the green grass was a lonely baseball: missed. Sam was devastated.

Now that the boys were spread out, Tommy Lee could no longer control everyone voicing their opinions. They let it all out, holding nothing back. They griped about how much time was being wasted and that the least they could have asked for was someone who could catch a fly ball. Billy even went as far as to declare they might as well invite the Widow Hayes to play.

"I say we give up this whole stupid game idea and just fight them mob boys! Whoever whoops the other teams' behinds to a bloody pulp first wins the diamond!" Fist asserted.

"I'm with you on that!" Boston agreed.

"Me too. It's the only choice we got now," stated Philly. "There is no way we can play against them mob boys."

"We're gonna get creamed," Charlie declared wiping the sweat from his brow.

Each remark impacted Sam to such a degree that if there hadn't been so many pairs of staring eyes, he would have broke into tears.

Tommy Lee ordered them to be quiet! "Don't y'all think you're being a bit dramatic? He missed one catch. Geez, it's his first time tryin'. The boy at least deserves some credit for that. He also deserves another chance before y'all jump down his skin like that. Sam, throw the ball to Charlie at first base please."

Sam picked up the ball and threw it the best he could to first base. To everyone's surprise, the aim was perfect as the ball drove hard into Charlie's mitt. In fact, the landing stung the center of his palm!

"Thank the Lord, that's one less thing we have to work on," Tommy Lee thought to himself. "Now Charlie, go on and throw the ball back to Sam."

"Come on! We ain't here to play catch!" Philly protested.

Tommy Lee ignored Philly and gestured Charlie to throw the ball to Sam.

It was a good throw on Charlie's part. Sam tried his best; he positioned his stance correctly and held the glove out in front of his chest, but when the ball reached the inside of his glove, he forgot to close the mitt. The ball just bounced out from the socket and fell to the ground.

"That does it." Philly tore off his catcher's mask in a fit of frustration.

"Hold on there Philly," ordered Tommy Lee. "I got an idea. Jimmy, Skip, be ready! Sam, throw the ball to Billy this time."

Sam examined the distance between him and the mound and prepared the ball at the tips of his fingers. In one gigantic swoop, he reared back and launched it forward. The ball bounced once just before the mound and hopped right into Billy's mitt.

"Attaboy! Nice throw!" Tommy Lee congratulated.

The boys were mildly amused. Billy pitched in a fastball and Tommy Lee, again, sent it high into center field. Jimmy and Skip exchanged puzzled expressions, wondering why Sam was just standing there, looking lost. Like bullets from a shotgun, the two boys simultaneously took off towards one another with their heads up and mitts out. They came in so fast that it appeared that they were going to collide. "I got it!" Skip cried out. Upon hearing this, Jimmy dashed out of Skip's path. Skip came in running hard. He stretched his arm out as far as it would go and, within a second before the ball would have touched the ground, Skip snagged it tightly with the tips of his glove. A thunderous applause followed. Skip looked over and with a smile, held up his glove for all to see.

Tommy Lee was impressed but felt this set up exposed too high a risk of collision so he switched Jimmy and Sam. Now Jimmy was in charge with both right and center field, areas where he felt quite competent.

Now it was time to see Sam swing the bat. Tommy Lee began by instructing Sam the team's only lefty, on proper grip and foot position. Next came the shift of body weight and the follow through. Once Sam was comfortable with each step, Tommy Lee showed him how to make them all flow together. The rest of the boys stood by impatiently. To them, Tommy Lee's batting lesson seemed futile. Although Sam had his rhythm down, every time he followed through, he lost all balance.

"Concentrate on keepin' your left foot planted dead to the ground," Tommy Lee suggested.

Sam glanced down at his left foot and nodded. He took another practice swing, this time managing to keep a steady balance. After a dozen more, Tommy Lee could see that this boy possessed some serious natural batting talent. "Nice job!" Tommy Lee encouraged and decided that Sam was ready for a pitch.

"Now remember, keep your eye perfectly on the ball at all times. Watch every move it makes and right when you think it's just a second too early to swing . . . swing."

Sam nodded attentively and repeated the instructions in his head. Meanwhile, Tommy Lee asked Billy for a gentle underhand delivery. Billy shook his head back and forth, disgusted at Tommy Lee's request for an underhand delivery. He wound up for the underhand pitch and sent it right down the middle. The ball came in slowly, over the plate, but Sam never swung at it; he forgot to.

"What happened?" Tommy Lee asked in a calm voice.

"I wasn't sure, I, uh . . ."

"I know. It's hard to tell when sometimes. How about this, Billy's gonna send you another pitch, only this time it'll be over hand and a fast one. Now I want you to watch the ball, but forget about deciding on when to swing. Just listen for my clap." Tommy Lee demonstrated once. "When you hear that, give it everything you got. Okay?"

Sam nodded and readied himself for the pitch. Billy was hesitant about delivering a fastball, but then realized he didn't care. If the ball hit the boy then it hit the boy. It wouldn't be his fault. As Billy wound up, Sam reminded himself over and over to wait for the clap, but when Tommy Lee did so, Sam was still busy reminding himself and didn't hear it. This resulted in another strike and the boys collectively snorted with laughter. Tommy Lee told Sam to ignore them. On the third try, Sam listened more closely and as soon as the clap came, he transferred all his energy to his upper body and swung the bat. *Whack!* Sam made contact and the ball dribbled out between first and second base. Billy missed the catch on a hop so second base man Charlie hurried in for the rescue.

"Run boy!" Tommy Lee exclaimed, waving him on to first base.

The connection left Sam in total shock. "Oh my gosh! First base!" he remembered and darted off. Charlie scooped up the ball but before he could spin around to flip it to Boston, Sam was safe on first. The most tremendous hush ever imaginable settled down over the diamond at that very moment. It was going to take a while for everyone to digest what had just happened. This kid could really run! Tommy Lee hurried out to first base and gave Sam a high five. The boys were beginning to whistle another tune now.

The afternoon sun was starting to sink beneath the brilliant green tops of the forest trees and Tommy Lee offered to walk Sam home. Tommy Lee knew today was Whitey's last day in town so he said his goodbye with a firm hug and tugged down on Whitey's lucky cap. Whitey was saddened by this moment that had finally come. He hardly had any time to process the impact this relocation would have, but understood that his life would never be the same again without these friends.

A crowd of familiar faces stood in the Greenburg's driveway, saying their goodbyes when the boys approached. Whitey looked around at all his friends with tearful eyes. "Before I forget," Whitey said to Billy. "I want you to have this." Whitey took off his St. Louis Cardinals cap and handed it to Billy.

"This is your lucky cap. I can't . . ."

"I want you to have it." Whitey gave Billy and all the other boys a hug. "Y'all better win that game. Ya hear!" He made his friends promise.

Whitey was angry as he walked up the driveway and got into the car. He wished his parents hadn't kept this a secret from him. He was growing up and in just a few years would be a man. When would his parents finally begin treating him like one? Whitey thought of Billy and the conversations they'd recently had of how Billy felt more and more as though life was becoming a race to keep up with Jimmy. Billy confided in Whitey with these feelings of inferiority and every time they talked their bond grew deeper. Whitey was just beginning to envision a strong and eminent friendship that could last forever. But now, going forward, there would be no more talks. Now long distance would take over and certainly drift the two boys apart.

The boys watched as the shiny black Ford backed out into the street and gently rolled out of sight.

On Sunday, both Pastor Cook and Coach Fleming finally agreed to being umpires and Tommy Lee took Sam down to the schoolyard to begin mobilizing his fielding skills.

Throughout that week, Tommy Lee put the boys' talents through a rigorous schedule of practice. He even brought in nine junior and senior high boys to act as an opposing team so that the boys could simulate actual games, and thereby more effectively practice their roles. By the end of day two, teamwork was happening! The boys were capitalizing on Tommy Lee's wisdom and developing some of their own.

Wednesday was dedicated to drafting the team's official batting order. After hours of deliberation, Tommy Lee made his decisions: Boston would bat first, since he could be most trusted to get a base hit. T.J. was reliably skilled at putting the ball in play and he was quick enough to reach first base on a tough infield ground ball, but Tommy Lee was hesitant to place him so early in the order. He knew going in that T.J.'s presence would, most likely, trigger extra drama from the mob. So Tommy Lee thought it was best to move T.J. later in the order to avoid early tension in the game. Charlie was skilled at bunting and also quite fast so Tommy Lee placed Charlie second in the team's batting order. This way, when a sacrifice bunt was needed, Charlie could pull through. There was no question of who would bat third. The third batter was always the team's best hitter, so Jimmy fit this slot perfectly. Skip was their cleanup power hitter and T.J. who was both a strong hitter and daring base runner, batted fifth. Sixth in the order was Sam, who was a very fast runner. Tommy Lee made certain to train him with a clear understanding of when and how to steal bases. If he could swipe second, there would be more of a chance to score a run. At the bottom of the order were Billy and Fist, who both had moderate agility with the bat and hitting ninth was Phillip Tupper. Although Philly might be quick with his mouth he was slow on his feet.

Thursday and Friday were full-fledged practice games against Tommy Lee's buddies. More and more, the boys were taking a liking to Sam. He was still very timid, but one can only expect as much when having to compete with the mouths of Philly, Boston, and Fist. Everyone was surprised that the mob hadn't come by to try and reclaim Sam. Still, even if they did, it was quite clear to the boys that Sam would never return to hanging out with the mob ever again. The boys wondered why Sam started and continued hanging out with a group of kids who treated him so bad, regardless of being promised to play or not. Skip was determined to find the missing pieces to the Sam/Slave puzzle. He wasn't sure how or where to begin and he was instinctually concerned for what the truth might uncover.

As it was becoming an extra hot day, Tommy Lee decided he didn't want to exhaust the boys any further, so he called quits and sent them home. Sam went his own way and the rest of the boys wondered how they would entertain themselves for the remainder of the day. As they passed through town they noticed a group of three girls in the empty field beside Charlie's house picking dandelions.

"Ain't that your property?" Philly pointed out to Charlie. "You should tell them to get."

"Someone's always there picking dandelions," said Charlie.

"What the heck for?" Boston asked.

"Dandelion salad. Don't you Yankees know anything?" Charlie recognized the girls from his school and church.

"That's disgusting." Boston cringed.

The three girls stood up from picking and giggled as the boys came closer up the road. They glanced for a moment and as the boys stared back, not a word was spoken. It felt like a slow-moving motion picture show. They all recognized one another through years of school and church but Fist tried acting like he'd never seen the three girls before in his life. He gripped the baseball he'd been holding in his mitt and thought to himself how amusing it would be to throw the ball at the girls and scare them off. But instead he behaved himself knowing he'd surely get a lecture from Skip. The girls looked away for a moment but then glanced back once the boys had passed. Fist looked back at the girls who's faces then became flushed with embarrassment for being caught looking and they turned to look away. Fist couldn't take the staring any longer. He stopped in his tracks and blurted out: "What the heck are y'all starin' at?" Skip spun around with a horrified look only to be more aghast as Fist worked up a mouthful of spit and hurled it as far as he could at the girls.

The boys all stopped frozen in their tracks. They were speechless. The girls were so disgusted they were unable to think of an appropriate response.

"What's gotten into you boy?" Charlie snapped and before Fist could further embarrass everyone, Charlie pulled him forward as fast as he could. The rest of the boys followed.

"Me?!" Fist was ready to defend his actions. "I don't need no bunch of girls starin' me down. You're lucky I don't go back there and give them something to really stare at!" Fist grabbed his crotch as he made this announcement.

Skip's jaw dropped. He was appalled. "Who on God's Earth taught you that?"

Fist looked away, shrugging his shoulders. "I dunno."

"They weren't starin' at you Fist. Trust me, they was starin' at me," Charlie informed him.

"Naw they weren't," said Billy. "All four of them was lookin' me up and down. I know that for a fact."

With this, Jimmy thought to himself: "Well, if they was starin' at you, Billy, I'm sure they was checking me out just the same."

Fist leaned back and gave Charlie and Billy a once over. "Why you both getting so defensive?" he wanted to know. "Since when do you care what any girls lookin' at?"

Charlie let out a sigh of frustration. It was too hot out and he was not in the mood to admit to Fist what was truly going through his mind regarding the girls. "I don't care Fist," he insisted. "But I don't need you upsettin' a bunch of lousy girls right outside my house for them to go knockin' on my front door wantin' to tell my mama and daddy about what you done."

Fist had nothing to counter with.

"Y'all wanna come to my house and get some lemonade?" Philly offered.

The boys were sweating hot. Lemonade sounded like the perfect remedy. Plus, they were anxious about tomorrow's game so sticking together was more comforting than just parting ways and heading home.

On the way, Skip decided it was time to insist that Jimmy and Billy come clean with whatever had them so recently preoccupied. At first, Billy waited for Jimmy to proceed but after it was obvious that Jimmy was too nervous to talk about it, Billy blurted out, "How long do we gotta wait to get an erection around here?"

Skip, Charlie and Philly could not believe their ears. Fortunately, there was no one around to hear what Billy said.

"You mean neither of you ain't never gotten a hard-on yet?" Skip asked in a quiet voice.

"Nope! Nothin' goin' on here," announced Billy.

"Damn! Y'all are late boner bloomers," Skip declared with a chuckle.

Charlie, Philly, Boston and Fist all burst into laughter.

"Get it?" Skip asked the twins, who just stood there looking confused. "Boner bloomers."

"I was eleven when mine first started comin'," Charlie was proud to announce.

"Can we find some other place to talk about this?" Jimmy requested.

Skip agreed with Jimmy that standing in the middle of Green Valley Drive was not the appropriate place for this discussion so he motioned for it be tabled until they could reach more private surroundings. Once they reached Philly's house, Mrs. Tupper served them each a glass of lemonade and the boys retired to the garage. The garage felt cool inside and there were empty egg crates for the boys to turn upside down and sit on.

Jimmy resumed the puberty topic with the following question: "So, I got another question. Where exactly do y'all put it when you get one?"

"Yeah, it does get a little annoying," responded Charlie with a nod of his head.

"A little?" Billy almost choked on his words. "Are you kiddin' me? I have tried to figure this out and . . . I don't know y'all? You can't just hide something like that. So what are you supposed to do? You supposed to wrap it around your leg or," Billy paused for a moment to think and then continued, "what were you sayin' the other day Jimmy? What's that stuff called?"

"Duct tape," Jimmy stated with wide eyes.

"Waitaminute," Skip began. "Just how big do you expect it's gonna get?"

Jimmy and Billy looked at each other and then Jimmy raised his arm and pointed along the length of his forearm.

"At least," Billy declared.

The facial expressions of Boston and Fist were a mixture of fear and shock while Skip, Charlie and Philly began to laugh.

"You warned me this could start happenin' Skip, but Holy Mackerel, you never said it would be like that."

"Where y'all gettin' this idea from anyhow?" Skip asked.

The twins told the boys about their staggering encounter with the aroused horse at Farmer Hayes's barn. Skip, then, understood why Jimmy and Billy were freaking out and was quick to clear up their naïve and inflated misunderstanding. Next, Skip tried to ease the twins' "late boner bloomer" trepidations. It took him almost until suppertime, but as soon as some progress was accomplished Jimmy and Billy were in much better spirits.

As expected with any small town, word about tomorrow's game had spread like wildfire. In no time, it seemed that every soul in Eugene would be there to watch. The mothers and the fathers of all the boys would be there, except for T.J's and Sam's. T.J. would be the only Negro there and the whereabouts of Sam's mom remained a mystery.

10

The game was scheduled to begin at three o'clock that Friday, July 4th and all of summer and its heat were in full bloom. The twins polished off a hearty breakfast before Skip swung by to pick them up. They rushed off to pick up the others and head to the baseball diamond for some pre-game practice. Tommy Lee arrived at two o'clock with Pastor Cook and Coach Fleming, who brought along his son's old catcher's mitt for Philly. Billy threw a dozen or so pitches to enable Philly to get used to the much bulkier and more padded mitt. Philly loved the way the mitt felt, for if he hadn't Tommy Lee would have preferred him to stick with what he was accustomed to. But Philly adapted to it immediately.

Meanwhile, a short procession of townspeople arrived and more were starting to trickle in and fill the bleachers. T.J. looked out at the sea of white folk. He knew no one from Slytown would be there, not even his own mom and dad. They didn't even know about the game. For if they had, they would have certainly forbade him from being there.

Pastor Cook was also examining the crowd. He was on high alert for what might come of their reaction to T.J.'s presence and sure enough there arose a disturbing spectacle. Pastor Cook motioned for Coach Fleming and they both approached the adult crowd to try and keep the disturbance contained but their efforts were squashed by the party's ringleader: "I suppose next time you'll be askin' for these coloreds to be allowed into our churches," said one of the fathers of the mob. Others from the crowd chimed in with offensive comments that ripped through T.J's ears like a dagger. Jimmy and Billy were standing closest to T.J. at the time. They looked over at him with compassion. They wanted to speak up against the adults but figured they better leave that job to either Pastor Cook or the coach. T.J. kept his head up but his eyes couldn't look at anything higher than the ground.

"You sure you're up for this?" Jimmy asked T.J.

"Don't let 'em get the better of you T.J." Billy said. "Ain't not one of them worth it."

T.J. nodded. The twins walked over and both put their arms around T.J.

"Hey! Look at that!" shouted Mr. Boyd from the crowd. "Hey McGee! Looks like your boys are sweet on that colored!"

Jimmy and Billy looked at one another with rage. They wanted so badly to clobber those men for their ignorance but Skip and Tommy Lee stepped up and made eye contact with each of them. "Don't even think about it," Tommy Lee warned them.

Jimmy looked over Tommy Lee's shoulder. "Looks like we don't have to. Billy, look at Daddy," he responded and motioned for Billy, Tommy Lee, Skip and T.J. to turn around.

Tom McGee was standing up and glaring hard at Mr. Boyd. "Watch what you say about my sons, Royce!" Ellen stood up and rested her calm hand upon Tom's broad shoulder. Tom took a deep breath. Hoyt, the milkman, came between them in an effort to keep the peace but Royce became aggressive. That's when Pastor Cook stepped in.

"Now gentlemen, let's all please settle down here for just a moment. There ain't no reason to fuss over this young boy bein' here. He's a child of God. Just like every one of y'all. And, I know these here boys were strapped for enough players their own age to form a team. Royce, Tom, both y'all are intelligent men. Everyone here knows that about you's! And I know you've been around these boys long enough to have seen that this here youngin's been playin' ball with them for years now. So, let's get it together. Especially knowing how much this here community respects the two of you. I'd expect something better out of the both of you's! In fact, I'd expect only the best out of every single person here. What almost occurred between the two of you's, just now, is not how God meant for us to be." Pastor Cook knew he could not tackle all the dissenters and win. He would have their attention for so few minutes; and if lost, no one, not even he, could get control of what was moving towards a dangerous conclusion. So in his common genius he spoke to everyone through Tom and Mr. Boyd. He knew just how to appeal to their pride with just the right amount of warm, but firm favorable attention without their feeling any more than a gentle pat on the back. And he took the others, outspoken as they were, out of the equation and gave them all a chance to calm down and to save face by focusing their attention singularly on the two men. Now, however the two men reacted, hopefully would be a calming cue to the others that the incident was resolved.

Meanwhile, the mob paraded into the schoolyard like Sherman into Atlanta.

Pastor Cook pulled out his pocket watch to verify that the mob was on time. "We're here to watch a ballgame folks," Pastor Cook reminded everyone. "We're not here to start a war. So let's all just relax and let these here boys have some fun."

Following the mob were two sturdy, middle-aged men wearing umpire black. Skip and the others immediately noted that these umpires were not local townsmen, which shook their nerves.

"T.J.'s a goner," Jimmy whispered to Billy. The tone in his voice was full of despair. "I knew this whole thing was a mistake."

Pastor Cook gathered everyone's attention for a short pre-game prayer.

As soon as he said Amen, Boston was ready to get things started. He exhaled his nerves and with a loud clap of his hands declared: "Alrighty boys! Let's do it up!"

"Hold up a second!" Sampson hollered.

Jonas had something to say. "Seein's how we're the guests and all, don't forget it's only fair that my team bat's first."

Coach Fleming agreed and everyone took their places: the boys in the field and the mob on the bench. Felix, a bony-looking worm with an army cut, stepped up to the plate and surveyed the entire field with his squinty eyes. As Felix pursed his lips and savored the view of the soon to be his baseball diamond he suddenly noticed the twig of a figure heading out to right field.

"Hey Jonas. Come here," he waved, stepping away from the box.

"What?" Jonas sounded annoyed.

"Get over here!" Felix clenched his teeth.

Jonas shook his head with irritation and came out from behind the fence to hear the secret.

"Look out there," Felix motioned with his head and eyes.

"Out where?"

"Out in right field. Do you see what I'm seein'?"

Jonas looked in the direction that Felix instructed and it took him only a second to realize why Felix was acting so edgy. "Sonuvabitch," he muttered. Jonas was in shock. He examined all the other players in the field, trying to piece the puzzle together. "Greenburg," he uttered. "Whitey Greenburg's missin'."

"Oh yeah, where's he at?" Felix wondered.

"I dunno. But him missin' seems real strange to me."

"Whatcha gonna do Jonas?" Felix asked. "We can't play against a girl."

Sampson and Morgan came from around the fence. "What's the matter?"

"Take a look for yourselves," Jonas pointed out. "Them boys talked my sister Sam in joinin' their team."

"What? You gotta be kiddin' me," questioned Morgan.

Jonas was fuming now.

By now, Coach Fleming was curious about the hold up. "What's goin' on boys?" he wanted to know.

"Coach, T.J's one thing but there ain't no way we're dealin' with that," Sampson told Coach Fleming.

"With what?" Coach Fleming was confused. Aside from T.J. what else was the mob objecting to?

"It's nothin' Coach," Jonas explained to the coach, before Sampson could speak. "We'll be fine, we're fine." Jonas told Felix, Morgan and Sampson to follow him as he returned to the bench and filled the rest of his boys in on the dirt. Ultimately, his conclusion was that "if them boys are fool enough to let a girl be on their team then so be it. I mean, think about it. My sister's never played a game of baseball ever before in her life, so what good is she gonna be to them? Especially, in right field with me and Morgan as lefties they must have been real desperate. We're gonna pulverize these boys!" Jonas slapped Sampson's back to emphasize his point, and the others nodded in agreement. "There's just one thing we gotta do," Jonas gathered them in closer. "We gotta keep Sam bein' a girl on the hush. Something here tells me them idiots ain't got no clue about him actually being a her."

"You mean, she's got them thinkin' she's a boy?" Glenn asked.

"Exactly!"

Sampson chuckled with arrogance "How dumb can them boys be. This here's gonna be a shutout fellas!" he stated. "Consider this field to be ours!"

Meanwhile, Tommy Lee and the others had become curious over the mob's private discussion. "Let's go already!" screamed Boston.

The mob returned to their seats and Coach Fleming declared: "Play ball!"

The boys put on their game faces and readied their defenses while the mob let out one annoyingly loud Whoop! in support of Felix. Philly watched for Tommy Lee's signal and dropped one finger to call for a fastball. Before Billy wound up, he lifted Whitey's lucky Cardinals cap from his head and secured it back on, only tighter. He pictured Jonas's face in the center of Philly's mitt and fired one right down the middle. Felix calculated the right perfect moment and then swung with all his might. The bat and ball connected in a clean line drive up the middle. Charlie moved in and grabbed it up on the hop. He made a quick pivot to the left and backhanded the ball to Boston, but Felix beat the throw.

With Felix on first, the next batter up was Rusty. Rusty had yellow teeth and bad breath. He had especially earned the twins contempt when his older brother, Sid, used to chase them home from school when they were nine. Back then, "the mob" had not yet formed, but Rusty had already demonstrated his obnoxiousness when he had tagged alongside his brother and laughed the entire way. Mrs. Hayes had been the first to spot the bullying and put a stop to it with one phone call to Rusty and Sid's mother.

Rusty fouled off the first two pitches and then hit a third-pitch pop fly into T.J's glove. Enraged by the circumstances, he flipped T.J. his middle finger and was about to shout a vile word but Coach Fleming stopped him. The coach was the only one who saw Rusty's inappropriate action and threatened a permanent bench sentence if he acted up again.

With one out and a runner on first base, Jonas swaggered up to the batter's box. After just one practice swing, he unloaded a first-pitch fly to the gap in the right. Jonas figured by the time the opposing teams' outfielders scrambled to it, he'd have time to reached third base and Felix would be home. Jonas dropped the bat and headed for first base and Felix left first and bolted towards second.

Jimmy took off for the ball. In no time, Jonas cleared first base and continued on to second with Felix on his way to third. Just before reaching the bag, Felix glanced back into right field. Jimmy had every inch of his arm extended for the catch. Jonas passed second and waved for Felix to run home, but Felix was not responding. The ball was falling fast but Jimmy was closing in. Both Felix and Jonas turned their heads just in time to watch as the ball landed safely in Jimmy's outstretched glove.

Felix had just rounded second so he would have to hustle if he was going to avoid a double play and the third out. With the crowd at the edge of their seats, the boys hollered for Jimmy to throw the ball to first. Jimmy surveyed the distance between him and Boston. It was much too far for his arm to cover alone. But Charlie had already read Jimmy's mind and was heading toward Jimmy to take the cut-off throw. Jimmy's throw hit the target and Charlie flung it on to Boston at first base. Boston was standing with one foot on the bag and the other stretched three feet in front. Charlie's throw arrived just before Felix could make that last stride to safety . . . . Bam! Just like that, a double play!

"That's three!" Coach Fleming announced.

The mob started swearing from the bench. Coach Fleming and Pastor Cook kept their eyes peeled for any attempts at confrontation as the mob crossed paths with the boys to take the field.

Sampson was the mob's pitcher. He stood tall as Jonas, but leaner. He wore a St. Louis Cardinals cap that fit just perfectly over his short, light brown hair. He stepped up to the mound like he was king and examined every move Boston made as he settled up to the plate. Jonas, of course, elected himself as catcher so he'd be right there to call all the shots.

Boston was not at all alarmed by Sampson's swagger and led off the bottom of the inning with an easy single on the opening pitch. He cheered himself all the way to first base and then spat on first baseman Rusty's shoe once he got there; which almost started a fight right there. Charlie, up next, spent more time taking practice swings than looking at live pitches; he later told Tommy Lee it was his own strategy to disrupt the pitcher's concentration. While Charlie was determined not to let any of Sampson's fastballs get by him, Jonas called for two curves and a drop.

"You'll get 'em next time," Tommy Lee assured Charlie, who sauntered back to the bench after striking out.

Next up was Jimmy McGee. He hovered over the plate and took a few sharp practice cuts with the bat. Sampson kept an eye on first and fired the ball to Rusty to keep Boston close. The first pitch to Jimmy was down and in. Jimmy swung off-stride and Coach Fleming hollered: "Strike one!" The second pitch was high and tight and Jimmy played it smart and laid off. "Ball one." The third delivery was identical to the first, only this time, Jimmy made contact. He knocked a solid single into left field, which nearly took off the shortstop's glove as he tried to snag it. Jimmy ran for first and Boston advanced to second. They wanted to go further, but Billy Maddox had the ball and was ready to throw an out from left field.

With one out and runners at first and second base, Skip came to bat and quickly lined the first pitch just fair inside the first base foul line. Boston and Jimmy took off and Lil' Denny, the mob's right fielder, quickly picked up the grounder and flipped it to Rusty at first but Skip had already slid one foot into safety! Rusty checked the status of the other runners. Jimmy was standing safe on second; but Boston had already rounded third base and was barreling home, eyes closed and head down. Rusty shot around and launched the ball to Jonas who tagged Boston for the second out. The boys now had runners on first and second with two outs and T.J. up to bat.

T.J. approached the plate. His stomach was knotted with fear and his limbs were frozen. He was too frightened to consider taking a practice swing. So he lifted the bat low behind his head and settled into the first stance he could find. This was not normal behavior for T.J. Tommy Lee and the boys were highly concerned.

"Keep your head up, you're never gonna see the pitch," Tommy Lee instructed nervously.

T.J. tried hard to obey Tommy Lee's advice, but could not find the strength. Right away, Sampson's arms dropped to his side and he stepped to the front of the mound. Skip took notice of Sampson's expression and stood up from the bench. "This can't be happening," he said to himself, shaking his head. He knew exactly what was on Sampson's hateful mind. The secret-plan Skip and the boys had worked so desperately to keep from T.J. was about to be blown wide open. Skip tried to think of something to say, but drew a blank.

All too soon, Sampson blurted out: "Hey! This warn't part of y'alls contract."

"Yeah, we ain't pitchin' to him," Lil' Denny joined in.

"Why not?!" Boston voiced.

"Shut up Yankee!" snapped Morgan.

"Are you kidding me with this? I'm going out there right now," announced Boston. "Fist! Come on!"

Right away, Fist was on his feet and ready to charge.

"Both of you's sit down!" Skip ordered firmly. "Tommy Lee, can you come with me please?" Skip hustled out to the mound and Jonas and Tommy Lee followed.

Skip knew that every detail regarding T.J.'s "contract" would be revealed if he did not calm Sampson down. Coach Fleming figured he better call time. Sampson, Jonas and Skip were quite a display of finger pointing and fury as Skip was confounded by Sampson's wicked imagination. Sampson asserted that if T.J. touched the bat it would, in turn, touch the ball he would later be throwing. Skip and Tommy Lee did all they could to quiet Sampson and Jonas's increasingly vile language toward T.J. The hatred rang loud and clear in T.J.'s ears and his head noticeably drooped.

"He has to bat Jonas. We'll only have eight batters without him," Skip tried to reason. "I don't get what the big deal is anyway?! He's just a boy, same as any of you."

"Not even close," Sampson fumed.

"Just 'cause his skin's a different color? Your skin's a different color than his but you don't hear none of his folk complainin'."

"Well duh! They're coloreds! Ain't nobody gonna listen to what they say." Jonas exclaimed.

By now, it was clear to Coach Fleming that this game had been a mistake from the beginning. He called the other umpires over and declared an early end. Skip did all he could to beg them to change their minds, but Fleming was already calling for both teams to gather up so he could make the announcement. Skip looked to Tommy Lee for some backup.

"So who's gettin' skunked here?" Skip wanted to know. "Coach, if we don't beat these boys fair and square, they're gonna be here everyday thinkin' this diamond is theirs."

"So then y'all will have to grow up some and learn to share the diamond." Coach Fleming stated firmly.

Tommy Lee knew this was not a realistic option. "That's gonna cause the town a mess of trouble Coach," Tommy Lee tried to reason. "These boys are incapable of bein' civil. There will be fightin' here every day if that happens." Tommy Lee leaned into Coach Fleming's ear and whispered: "The only way to make this whole thing seem fair in their world is to let them play for it. They're just kids. So that's what makes sense to them right now."

Coach Fleming looked out into the bleachers, where members of the crowd were expressing divided opinions. He worried that there were not enough tolerant people there to support T.J. Yet, at the same time, having been a boy once himself, he understood Tommy Lee's argument. These two groups of boys were clearly not mature enough to verbally negotiate a settlement, even with some adult help. The coach looked at Sampson and Jonas and raised one finger in warning. "Any wild moves and I'll have the sheriff arrest you's both. Is that clear?" Sampson and Jonas both nodded and Coach Fleming permitted the game to resume.

As Sampson returned to the mound, Jonas followed close behind and whispered, "Trust me Sampson. I agree with you. That boy's got his comin'. But today it's about our gettin' this ball field."

Tommy Lee and the team all walked T.J. to the batter's box. Their hearts all reached to T.J. as they each felt a surrendering of their own innocence. Although they had each witnessed displays of bigotry throughout their youth, this time they felt responsible for it. Perhaps they should have listened to Jimmy's warning and found some way to find a replacement for T.J. They allowed their own greed over the diamond to get in the way of their better judgment of a friend's feelings and personal safety.

T.J. picked up the bat and before settling into his stance Tommy Lee asked if he was okay with continuing on.

T.J. looked at Tommy Lee with brave eyes. "You think Ah didn't expect dem boys to treat me like dis?"

Hearing this broke the boys' hearts.

Tommy Lee sighed and asked T.J. what he wanted to do. "You don't have to put up with them words if you don't want to. We can stop playin'."

"No way," T.J. replied. "Hearin' dem say it only makes me want to play all the more."

A feeling of tremendous pride came over the boys. They were beginning to understand a small sense of their friend's courage. Tommy Lee couldn't hold back a wry smile thinking this could become contagious.

Tommy Lee wrapped his arm around T.J.'s shoulder and leaned in. "I don't get it, but I get it," he said to him with a smile and the game resumed.

Sampson exhaled a huge cloud of anger and then whistled a fastball right down the middle of the plate and T.J. swung hard. The ball soared high into left field making T.J. feel good all over. Billy Maddox raced back, holding his mitt out in front of him, and made the catch. This was the third out and the first inning was over, with no runs scored.

Leading off the second inning for the mob was Tripp Parker, their shortstop and cleanup hitter. Fortunately for the boys, there was nothing for him to clean up. Billy threw in whatever pitch Philly called for without hesitation. On the one-and-two pitch, Tripp smashed a long liner into the gap in left field. Skip scrambled to get to it, but by the time he could make the throw, Tripp was safe on second base.

Next up was Morgan, the mob's third baseman and their other lefty. It was only by luck that Morgan knocked a blue darter clean past Charlie's knees. Jimmy ran in for the difficult catch. The ball bounced once and Jimmy snagged it on the hop, as Tripp advanced to third and Morgan held at first.

With two runners on bases and none out, second baseman Glenn Parker, Tripp's cousin, was up. Growing up, Glenn, the twins and Charlie Blair were friends, but after a misunderstanding around "missing" baseball cards, Glenn was convinced by his cousin to join the mob. Tommy Lee gave special instructions to hold Morgan on first, but after two change-ups, Glenn managed a ground ball up the middle. T.J. sprang to his left and snagged the ball. He launched it home and Tripp was out at home plate. And Morgan must have been daydreaming because he failed to advance to second on the throw home. His friends were quite vocal with their frustration over this, which he countered by stating that they should have called him on it during the play, not after. The next two batters, Lil' Denny and Billy Maddox, both struck out on high fastballs to end the top half of the inning.

As the boys came in from the field, they cheered Sam all the way up to the plate. Their appetites were peaked at the anticipation of seeing the mobs' socks blown off by their ex-ball retriever's thunderbolt-like running abilities. Unfortunately for Sam, she could not stop her knees from shaking. Tommy Lee diagnosed her with a case of rabbit ears and hurried over to offer some confidence. Tommy Lee knew the truth about Sam's gender. They had a long discussion about it the day he walked her home from practice. "There's nothin' to be scared of Sam," he whispered. "Remember what we talked about when I walked you home the other day? They're gonna try and rile you up. But don't you listen to 'em. Just play like we taught ya." Tommy Lee stepped away second-guessing his choice of Sam's place in the lineup. Perhaps she should have batted ninth.

Sam's first practice swing sent the mob into a ridiculous fit of laughter. They pointed and jeered, and, on the brink of tears, Sam started to retreat back to the bench. Tommy Lee stopped her halfway and whispered something into her ear. Sam nodded a few times and with a new poise, returned to the plate. The mob taunted her all the way through the first pitch, a swing and a miss, and before Sampson delivered his second, he mocked Sam with a series of blown kisses. She resisted, knowing what Tommy Lee had whispered was true. Her turn at bat needed to last as little time as possible. The longer she allowed it to be drawn out, the more opportunity the mob would have to reveal her gender, not only the crowd but more importantly her teammates. And she did not want that to happen. Tommy Lee had warned Sam that these newfound friends of hers were only based on the condition of them believing she was a boy. Eventually, they will learn the truth. And when they do, Tommy Lee explained that he had little confidence in their maturity-level for handling that truth. Sam understood that her relationship with these boys could be destined for doom. But all her life she had felt like "a nobody with no particular place in the world" and so her sole purpose for concealing her gender was the window of opportunity it provided her to be accepted and do something special, even if it only lasted a short nine innings.

With the count at two balls and two strikes, Sampson decided to give his arm muscles a rest. There seemed no point in laboring over this batter. The next delivery was a gopher ball that eased right down the middle in plain sight but Sam's lack of courage led to a swing and a miss. Every member of the mob laughed, including Jonas, the catcher. But their reaction proved to be a costly mistake as the ball slipped past Jonas's mitt and rolled between his legs. Suddenly, a crowd of voices began shouting: "Run!" Although Sam didn't understand why, she followed orders and in no time flat was on the bag. "Second!" the same voices urged. Sam looked back to find Jonas, scrambling in circles to locate the ball.

"Left!" Sampson barked.

Jonas turned and snatched it up. He made an accurate throw to second but it was too late. The mob stood humbly silent with their jaws dropped. A girl had just bested them. Samantha had reached second base on Jonas' passed ball.

"You never said she could run," Sampson whispered loud to Jonas. All Jonas could do was shrug his shoulders in disbelief.

Pastor Cook overheard this and looked Sam directly in the face. "I thought I recognized you, your Mia's girl, aren't you? I didn't see your mama here today? Will she be coming to the picnic?"

Sam quietly shook a nervous "no" at every word. It took him a moment, but he finally realized the implication. "Okay, I won't tell no one," he promised quietly and placed his pointer finger before his lips. "Mums' the word darlin'." Sam smiled in response.

The mob seemed unable to recover from their shock and after Billy's two practice swings he became impatient. "Heaven's to Geez! Let's get a move on!" Needless to say, Ellen was appalled and would have something to say about Billy's near-blasphemy later.

Sampson squeezed the ball tightly with the tips of his fingers and sent forth a glare before beginning the wind-up. He planned on throwing in some extra heat to stir Billy up. As his concentration was solely on the fastball, Sampson neglected to notice that Sam was nearly eight feet off the second base bag. Just as Sampson threw his arm forward, Sam made a mad dash for third base. Jonas saw the attempt and knew what he must do. Yet, not a moment after the ball slammed into the catcher's mitt, Sam was standing safely on third. The steal grabbed Billy's attention and resulted in a swing and a miss. "Strike one." Coach Fleming announced, but the boys didn't seem to care. They were all celebrating Sam and the mob was fuming.

The second pitch was far out of reach and Jonas had to stand up to snag it. After throwing it back, he looked to Tommy Lee who contemplated the situation and signaled back to call for an intentional walk. After three more outside deliveries, Billy stormed off to first base complaining about being robbed. This annoyed Rusty and the two started pushing each other. Fortunately, the umpire intervened before any jabs were thrown.

With no outs and two runners on, next up was "Fist" Bradshaw, and the mob was confident that no run would come of this at-bat. Fist over-swung on the first two pitches before Tommy Lee instructed him to slow down and take his mind off trying to kill the ball. Fist then scored a single when he lined the third pitch between first and second. Sam immediately took off for home and Jonas jumped to block the plate. Morgan caught the ball on a hop and spun around to throw in but stopped after seeing home plate blocked by a crowd of cheering opponents. The boys had just scored their first run of the game! Billy was one stride from second and, the slow running Fist was halfway to first. Rusty called for the ball and Morgan hurled it in time to make the putout on Fist at first base.

"Remember to keep your eye on the ball all the way through," Tommy Lee prompted Philly, who was approaching the plate with Billy on second and one out.

Philly stretched out both arms and took a haughty practice swing. He looked back at his proud family in the stands and smiled and waved. When ready, Sampson pitched in a clumsy knuckle ball. Philly swung on time and tapped a low rider towards first base. Sampson took off after it, but the ball inched its way past the foul line and landed in the grass.

"You're lettin' your shoulders drop. Keep 'em steady," Tommy Lee instructed. "Don't feel like you gotta crowd the plate either. Back up some."

"Yeah fatty! Back up some!" Jonas mocked.

Philly's mother was appalled by the comment and embarrassed for her son.

"Ignore him," Tommy Lee promptly instructed. "And you . . ." he looked down at Jonas. ". . . knock it off!"

Philly did everything he was told, but still couldn't manage a hit. Tommy Lee asked what was troubling him and for the first time in Philly Tupper's life he had no excuse. Everything Tommy Lee said he was doing wrong needed correction and he knew it. Philly's mother offered her sympathetic encouragement from the stands, which only embarrassed him further on his lonely journey back to the bench.

Boston took the plate, with two out, and fouled off the first two pitches. The third pitch: a fastball, headed up the middle and connected squarely on Boston's bat. Tripp took a mighty leap forward to snag the ball but it scooted under his stomach as he landed with a *splat!* Felix had already moved forward from centerfield and made the low catch. He then backhanded the ball and threw a strike to first that beat Boston by a nose. The second inning had ended but the boys had a miraculous 1-0 lead!

Top of the third and the mob was at the bottom of their order, with Sampson up first. He swung late at all three of Billy's fastballs. "I'll have to remember that for next time," both Tommy Lee and Billy thought to themselves.

Now the mob was back at the top of their order, with one out, and Felix blooped the first-pitch fastball into left. Jimmy fielded it on the bounce, holding Felix at first with a single. Rusty batted next and with Jonas on deck and Felix, the mob's self-proclaimed fastest runner and number-one base stealer standing on first, Tommy Lee requested a time out to discuss strategy.

It was too early to introduce Billy's curveball, which needed to be saved for later innings. But, if Rusty ended up earning a single and Felix did not get thrown out, then Felix would be at second or maybe even third, during Jonas's turn at bat. So, Tommy Lee instructed Billy to "sucker" Felix into attempting to steal second base with four wide pitches. Tommy Lee then motivated Philly to be quick enough on the draw with his throw to Charlie on second to put out Felix during his attempt.

Billy's first pitch to Rusty was a fastball way outside. In the process, Felix noticed that Billy was ignoring him at first base and readied up his feet and legs to steal second base.

As Billy threw his next pitch, Felix took off for what he thought was a sure steal of second base. As he ran, he couldn't help turn his head to watch Billy's pitch on its flight towards the plate. This slowed Felix up enough that Philly's throw to Charlie, on second, put Felix out by five feet—not even close. The boys celebrated as Felix huffed and puffed his entire way back to the bench.

After two balls and two strikes, Rusty middled a slow rolling single past third base that Charlie tried to field, but lost control and Rusty safely took first base. Next up was Jonas.

Billy ground his teeth and cut his eyes as Jonas settled into his stance. Jonas just laughed it off. Philly called for a sinker, which Billy questioned. This was not a strong pitch for him and the mob's star hitter was at the plate. Billy often turned his wrist too far, causing the ball to drop too soon. Well, he did just that and his first pitched sinker bounced in front of the plate.

"What the hell was that?!" Jonas complained.

"Careful with that mouth son," Coach Fleming warned sternly.

Predicting another sinker, Jonas was ready to step forward to adjust, if needed, but Billy threw a fastball and Jonas swung late.

The next pitch was a change-up and Jonas hit it off the end of the bat for a bloop double, down the right field line.

Tripp followed by knocking a double into no man's land that brought Rusty home. The mob had tied the score, and the team had one out left with a runner on second. Their next batter up was Glenn. Despite the setback, Billy remained cool and struck Glenn out on a series of fastballs and sliders.

Charlie led off the bottom of the third inning with a base hit. Next, Jonas debated whether to have Sampson walk Jimmy or attempt a strike out. With Skip on deck and T.J. in the hole, having runners on bases made it too risky, so he called for Sampson's sinker. Very few had ever managed to make the connection with this infamous pitch. It came in so calm and clean that batters couldn't help but lick their chops. But suddenly, out of nowhere, the ball would drop and the next thing that batters would hear was the disheartening sound of "slap" from the catcher's mitt while they swung aimlessly at thin air.

Sampson smiled as he reared back for the first delivery. The ball came down the middle, heading directly for the midpoint between Jimmy's knees and shoulders. "You've gotta be kiddin' me," he had enough time to say to himself. Jimmy couldn't believe that Sampson would be foolish enough to throw him a gopher ball with a runner on first. A rush of adrenaline shot through Jimmy's body as he took a full swing. He swung so hard he nearly did a three-sixty in the batter's box. He dropped the bat and was ready to run, but it dawned on him that his attempt was fruitless. Jimmy turned around and watched Jonas flash the ball before his eyes. Jimmy was dumbfounded. He looked to Coach Fleming, expecting Jonas to be charged with an error for having cheated, but all the coach said was: "Strike one!" Jimmy and his friends were speechless.

Jimmy looked over at Tommy Lee hoping for a time out. Tommy Lee called it and advised Jimmy not to swing at the second pitch but rather use the time to try and understand it. Jimmy tried hard to examine the second pitch but it seemed hopeless. It was clearly a sinker but a slow one? Jimmy had never heard of anything like this, not on the radio or even from reading monthly issues Sport magazine at the Delta General.

When the third pitch came in, Jimmy waited for the ball to get halfway to the plate and then took a step forward as Tommy Lee had suggested. Jimmy reached out and swung with everything he had. *Crack!* All of Jimmy's teammates stood up from the bench and cheered as the ball screamed into left field. Jimmy's blue eyes burst open and he took off toward first. He looked up and saw that the ball was still going. Jimmy couldn't believe it. This was going to be a home run!! Charlie hurried home to high fives and Jimmy circled the bases into the welcoming arms of an extremely proud Billy and the rest of the team. The boys were now in the lead by two! Tommy Lee's heart was racing.

Fueled by the team's sudden rush of success and the surprising vulnerability of the mob, Skip rocked a first-pitch blue darter into center that left Tripp handcuffed as the ball screamed by. With both Billy Maddox and Felix chasing down the ball, Skip had just enough extra time to safely reach second base.

T.J. took the plate and with every shout of approval from the boys and their fans, the mob's anger escalated. Sampson wound up for the pitch and with all his rage and disregard for Coach Fleming's ultimatum fired it directly at T.J. The ball struck T.J. in his left shoulder sending him to the ground. Everyone suddenly went numb.

"Oh my God!" Tommy Lee shuddered.

"This is exactly the sorta thing I knew would happen," Jimmy thought to himself.

"Hey!" Fist raged and leaped up into the backstop as if he was going to tear his way right through the fencing. It took the remainder of the team to rip him down.

"Time out!" Coach Fleming's face was red with heat as he rushed to T.J.'s aide, with Tommy Lee following.

"What are you trying to do pulling a stunt like that?!" Boston fumed and cursed out Sampson with his eyes.

"You best watch your mouth 'fore I's kick it in, Yankee!" Jonas snarled.

"Ohhh, I'm gonna tear every last one of you boys up!" Fist roared and stormed out from the dugout.

Mr. Bradshaw ordered Fist to calm down as he and the other worried men hurried onto the field. Back and forth the men debated the pros and cons of allowing the game to continue. The boys hurried over to check on T.J.

T.J. was still lying on the ground holding his burning shoulder. Skip and Tommy Lee helped him to sit up. Tommy Lee asked if he was able to move his arm. Coach Fleming heard T.J.'s moan and walked away from the men to check on T.J. T.J. cringed as he tried raising his arm and Coach Fleming applied gentle pressure on and around the point of impact. He asked T.J. to move it back and forth. Fleming and Tommy Lee could already see a good-size contusion beginning to appear.

"You're done T.J." Coach Fleming decided. He looked across at Tommy Lee. "This game is done. And I'm gonna have a word with the sheriff and Sampson's parents." Tommy Lee did not dare dispute the coach's cold resolve. "We need to get this boy back to Slytown with his own kind. He can't be here no more."

"Pleez sir, Ah's gotsta keep on playin'," said T.J. "Ah's can't be lettun' dese boys git da best of me, 'specially not now."

"No son, you need to have that arm looked at." Coach stood up and rejoined the men. Although it was clear that T.J. could no longer play, there was still the issue of how the conflict surrounding the boys' use of the diamond would be resolved.

T.J. was ashamed. The last thing he wanted to do was let his boys down. Although he had seriously worried about how this day would turn out, he never anticipated an early quit. The men were trying to figure out a way for the two groups of boys to share the diamond but nothing was satisfying the majority. T.J. looked up at his friends as they looked at Skip as if to say "stop this from happening!" Barely breathing, they all stood there as their fate was being decided just a few feet away. While Skip wasn't sure what to say, he still felt he should try and say something in his team's defense.

But it was too late, the circle of men broke and their attention turned to the two teams.

"I'm sorry boys," was all Coach Fleming needed to say.

"But Daddy!" Billy choked.

"This is how it's got to be son," Tom said with a sad tone. "It's for T.J.'s best interest and all of yours. Y'all are just gonna have to find another way."

The boys' hearts sank while Jonas and the mob members slyly smiled at one another. They knew if permitted to, at least, share the diamond it would only be a short time before their crude conduct would drive the boys out altogether.

Although the men agreed this case was closed and no longer open for discussion, the boys erupted with every argument they could think of. Meanwhile, T.J. noticed that the women had all gathered together in front of the bleachers. For a moment, one of the women and T.J. made accidental eye contact. She looked away from him with disgust and then down as if ashamed for her reaction. T.J. didn't know who she was; the only woman he recognized was Mrs. McGee. It was a struggle, but he rose to his feet and took long deep breaths as he worked his arm back into motion. He then walked over to the group of women and stood behind Ellen.

"Excuse me ma'am, may Ah ax you a question?" he said to Mrs. McGee.

Ellen turned around. Today, she had styled her medium length brown hair up in Victory Rolls. She was surprised to see T.J. standing there. Without hesitating she responded. "Of course hon'."

"Ma'am," T.J. swallowed the lump in his throat before he continued. "My name is T.J. ma'am."

A warm smile came across Ellen's entire face and her brown eyes were calm. "I know who you are sweetie."

T.J. nodded. Her response helped to reduce his anxiety. "If you please, would you mind tellin' dem men folk dat it's alright for me to play. Ah wanna play. Ah have to play." T.J. did not want to be defeated by the mob and their bigotry.

There was a long pause before Ellen replied. She could see the pain in T.J's eyes. Somehow, she understood the deeper meaning of what T.J. was saying. "Of course" was all she said and with a deep and vigorous breath she walked into the baseball diamond.

At first, Ellen's presence went ignored, even by Tom and the twins. Ellen spoke up louder and this time Pastor Cook quieted everyone down.

"So what'd y'all decide?" she asked, although she knew the answer.

Pastor Cook and Coach Fleming explained what had been decided.

"And y'all think everything's gonna work out just peachy, is that right?" There was a heavy hint of sarcastic doubt in Ellen's tone.

The men all nodded.

"Well, apparently, none of y'all live in the same town as these boys and I do. 'Cause I can tell y'all from experience that this here diamond, in less than a week, is gonna look like it was hit by a German fire-bomb run." Ellen's tone was strong. Her goal was only to generate results, not more arguments. Most of her appeal was to Mayor Armstrong with regards to the rough condition of the empty lot the mob boys were using.

Jonas was appalled by Ellen's claim, but just as quick as he was able to voice his objection, he was hushed by three quarters of the men for being rude. The fathers of the mob were also about to speak up on their son's behalf but Mayor Armstrong claimed the floor before they had a chance.

Mayor Armstrong requested a private dialog with the four umpires. He knew Ellen was right and so he had to figure out what to do to either ensure T.J.'s safety or find him a replacement. Plenty of other boys were available but, to remain fair, they would have to select someone within their age group and that was the dilemma: of the few remaining boys their age none of them knew how to play baseball. Pastor Cook and Coach Fleming, feeling partial to Skip's team, wanted to pick someone older that would boost their chance of winning. Of course, this opinion had to be kept under wraps, even though almost everyone else in town wanted to see Skip's team win as well. Another opinion was to give Tommy Lee's boys an automatic win as punishment to the mob for their foul and ignorant behavior.

As Ellen stood by listening, she shook her head in disappointment. She wondered why these men were not standing up for the justice of the matter. She saw the hopelessness behind the struggling determination in T.J.'s eyes. He was the victim and shouldn't have to be banned from playing. From Ellen's point of view, this town had an opportunity to do something good for a boy who, just because of the skin color he was born with, would suffer an entire life of eradicated opportunities. She raised her shoulders, took a deep breath and asked their permission to speak again. This time her argument focused on the matter of principle that "her team" should not be obstructed from using the exact same members they practiced with. Such a revision would disrupt their entire chemistry and inevitably set them up for failure.

Tom's heart filled with pride as he brought his right arm around Ellen's shoulders and pulled her in close. "Since when do you know so much about baseball?" He said with a smile and a wink.

Coach Fleming smiled and nodded. "Well gentlemen, I do believe Ellen makes a good point."

Pastor Cook agreed. He turned and acknowledged Ellen with a smile. "I believe we all could learn a thing or two from you ma'am. Tom, your wife's a blessing to this community."

As far as Pastor Cook and Coach Fleming were concerned, the decision to continue with the game was now made.

"I'll go check on the boy and if he's all right, then I think the boy should be allowed to play. Mayor?"

Mayor Armstrong and the majority of the men agreed and Coach Fleming walked over to Tommy Lee who was now beaming from ear to ear. "Hmm," said the coach, "I hope you're still smilin' after all this is through."

"Yes sir!" said Tommy Lee.

Coach Fleming walked up to T.J. and to the best of his knowledge and experience, assessed the stamina of T.J's arm.

"Tommy Lee, will you help T.J. out to his base? I'm goin' to have a talk with Sampson and Jonas," Coach Fleming said. "T.J., if that arm starts hurtin', you best let me know. You hear?"

T.J. earnestly nodded a yes.

By now, Jonas had decided to privately give Sampson a lecture. "Sampson, if it weren't obvious before that this town hates us, it sure as heck is now. You best not pull any more stunts like that or you're liable to get us all thrown outa here. Just play like we always play. We got this game beat. Okay?"

Sampson nodded.

When Coach Fleming arrived at the mound, Jonas spun around and gushed out a pathetic apology on behalf of Sampson. The coach told him to "save it" and began scolding Sampson like he had just committed mayhem. Sampson just stood there wearing a dumb expression and wishing his father would come over and have his back for once.

After Coach Fleming had made it clear that the mob was now on a short leash, finally, the game resumed. The boys were in the lead by two runs with Skip on second and T.J. on first. Sam was thrown out on three strikes and received the team's first out for their half of the inning. Billy snagged a base hit but Skip was thrown out before he could reach third base. The bottom of the third inning finished on Fist's out after he swung off-stride at the first two pitches, foul-tipped the third and popped the fourth pitch high up and down into Morgan's glove; they were all fastballs.

With the mob down by two at the top of the fourth inning, the boys became overconfident and their defense lost its focus, giving up two runs as the mob tied the game at 3-3. Despite both teams' best efforts the score remained tied for the rest of the fourth and through the fifth inning.

By the looks of things, Sampson then needed a rest from pitching so Jonas called on Glenn Parker for some relief. The boys loaded the bases with one out on Glenn's fastballs and splitters. But

Boston and Charlie struck out, stranding the runners, and the game was still tied by the end of inning number six.

In the seventh inning, Billy began moving the ball in and out, faster and slower, per Tommy Lee's advice, in an attempt to disrupt the batter's timing. This almost worked but Glenn drove the two-and-one pitch out past Skip, giving him a double and Lil' Denny, able to lay off the high ones, drew a walk. Next up to bat was Billy Maddox. The mob yelled out "Come on Maddox! Billy Madds! The Billaroo! Knock this one outa here!" and Billy Maddox smacked a long fly ball to left, but Skip caught it for the out. Billy Maddox reacted by throwing the bat down into the dirt and pouting his way back to the bench.

As Sampson stepped up to the plate, Billy replayed the opposing pitcher's vicious display of bigotry in his mind. Billy glared back at the runners on first and second and then ahead at Sampson. Billy channeled the enmity he was feeling against Sampson along with his frustration over the tied-up score into a boiling pot of strike-zone heat. Still, Sampson tipped a swift bouncer off toward Fist who positioned himself correctly for the catch. But the ball slipped past his glove, popped up over his head, and struck the dirt. Glenn flew hard past T.J. and slammed the side of his foot into the third base bag. Skip came charging in and managed to throw out Lil' Denny at second. Batters now stood on first and third with the mob back at the top of their order.

"Steerike one!" Coach Fleming trumpeted on Felix's swing and a miss. The next pitch was a slider, but Felix fought it off and smacked a humpback liner in the gap between second and third base. Seemingly out of nowhere, T.J. dove out and up at the same time and snagged the ball in the tip of his glove for the inning-saving third out! It was an impressive play and the crowd cheered with delight. Billy raised his left hand to high-five T.J. on their way in from the field. Jimmy and T.J. both noticed the intentional switch and asked Billy how his right arm was holding up.

"I'm glad our share of the inning's over. I need a rest but I'll be fine. Trust me."

Glenn Parker pitched only to Charlie, who collected a single. When Jimmy stood up to bat, Sampson returned as pitcher. This time, Sampson gave Jimmy his sinker with a little more speed which caused Jimmy to swing late. But Jimmy correctly assessed the next pitch and took a hefty swing, sending the ball just left of second base. Tripp dove headfirst in an attempt to make the catch but missed and Jimmy reached first base before the ball could be thrown!

"Way to go Ace!" Tommy Lee called to Jimmy. "Alright, Skip you're up. Hit us a homer."

Skip expected a sinker but Tommy Lee motioned to look out for a fastball. Conveniently, that was exactly what was thrown and Skip smacked a home run over the left field fence! Jonas tried hard to chase after it, but the fly ball wouldn't drop. The homer put the boys back in the lead 5-3!

T.J. collected a first-pitch single but Sam couldn't handle the mounting pressure and quickly struck out. Billy was up next and smacked a line drive through the left-center gap. Tommy Lee and the boys watched from the tips of their toes as Billy Maddox chased after the ball and snagged it up with the tip of his glove on its first hop. In the blink of an eye, Billy Maddox threw to second where Glenn Parker tagged T.J. for the out and then gunned the ball to first base, where Rusty put out Billy. Bam! Like choreographed clockwork, the mob made a double play that retired the seventh inning.

Although late, the arrival of the afternoon breeze was much appreciated by everyone. Pastor Cook's wife and some of the other mothers and daughters had gone off to fetch water for everyone. The crowd and umpires were all hungry but with just two innings to go, not a single player was calling for any sort of break. After water was served, all the mothers and daughters returned to their homes to finish preparing the food they were bringing to the annual Fourth of July picnic.

In the bottom of the eighth, the mob tied the game, once again, with a series of base hits that turned into runs. This left the boys desperate and Tommy Lee fidgety during their scoreless half of the eighth. Now, only one more inning should remain.

11

Pastor Cook looked up at the sun and wiped his brow. He wondered about the exact time and pulled out his pocket watch: ten minutes after five as the game entered the ninth inning tied at five runs apiece.

First up to bat for the mob was Sampson and the dreaded top of the order would follow. Sampson got lucky on the three-and-two pitch with a solid single to left field. Jimmy and Skip ran to the rescue but couldn't make the throw to Charlie in time to put Sampson out at first base.

Next up was Felix, batter number one in the mob's order. He warmed up with three overconfident practice cuts then quickly knocked a first-pitch lazy fly directly into Jimmy's glove. Sampson, knowing that time was running out in a tied game, had started to run for second on the flyout but scrambled safely back to first, beating Jimmy's heads-up throw just in time.

With one out, Rusty was up next. But Tommy Lee called time and started toward the pitcher's mound for another strategy session. Before he had made it halfway, Billy surmised what was on his mind.

Tommy Lee whispered into Billy's ear, "It's time to unleash the beast." The order sent chills up and down Billy's spine. "They're probably gonna have Rusty sacrifice bunt Sampson to second. But that's okay. It'll give us two outs. Then, it's time for your curveball—saved for Jonas—just like we talked about." Even though Billy remained poker-faced as Tommy Lee left the mound, his teammates knew exactly what was up. Billy leaned forward to read the zone.

The sun was beginning to shift west over the woods and away from the diamond. Everyone in the stands eagerly anticipated whatever was obviously up Tommy Lee's sleeve. The mob just sneered to show they were afraid of nothing.

Billy delivered pitch number one and Rusty did as expected and shortened up for the bunt. He tapped it towards first base. Sampson, who was already off the first base bag, went speeding towards second. Equally as fast, Billy raced from the pitcher's mound, snagged the ball on the second hop and threw to Boston at first. Rusty was out and Sampson had safely made it to second.

Now it was Jonas's turn. Jonas, and his usual arrogance, stepped up to the plate ready to devour whatever Billy could send him. He adjusted his brown tweed cap and settled into his stance. Billy worked up another hard gaze and lifted Whitey's Cardinals cap to wipe away the hours of sweat underneath. There was passion in how he gripped the ball and liveliness in the pivot of his windup. Billy lifted both arms high above his head and came down with a giant thrust of his right arm as he slung the first pitch toward home plate. The ball sliced through the air so wide off the plate that Jonas was convinced it would be outside. He then actually stepped away from the plate and never swung. The amazing pitch curved in at the last moment and fell belt-high right down the center of the plate. Billy commended himself with a private but highly energetic "Yes!"

"Steerike one!" Coach Fleming proclaimed.

"What?!" Jonas objected.

"That was strike one son."

Jonas was clearly in denial. "How's that?" he wanted to know, feeling disturbed. As Coach Fleming explained the ball's movement, Jonas replayed the previous few seconds in his prickly little mind. Jonas looked out at Billy and gritted his teeth. He tore off his cap and threw it in the dirt and took a deep breath as he ran his fingers through his thick, dark hair. Whatever had just happened, Jonas was not about to let it happen again. He would kill the next pitch.

But, as planned, Billy's next pitch was a perfect jewel, and fortunately, so was the third! Jonas swung hard and missed both times. He again questioned the umpire's judgment, but knew he had no other choice but to quietly crawl back to the bench, furious.

The rest of the mob just stood there behind the fence, totally confused as the boys stampeded in from the field ready to blast the hell out of whatever pitch and play the mob could produce.

"Batter up!" Coach Fleming sounded off as Charlie hurried in to grab the bat and prepare himself for a hit. Tommy Lee reminded everyone to settle back down and focus. The game was still tied and the boys needed to score at least one run.

Sampson did everything he could to strike Charlie out but couldn't. After Charlie's base hit, Jimmy, who had been stinging the ball all day, worked a walk.

With two runners on and no outs, there was a lot of pressure on Skip not to strike out. And he handled himself like a pro sending a bouncer that took a wild hop to Tripp's left. But the shortstop was able to make a brilliant play as he snagged the grounder and threw to third baseman Morgan, to get the lead runner Charlie at third.

With one out and runners at first and second, T.J. apprehensively fouled off the first two pitches but was able to lay off the next two to run the count even at 2-2. Jonas worried that Sampson might need relief as he looked to have nothing left. But, the next pitch broke sharply and T.J. swung off stride. "Strike three!" Fleming bellowed.

With two outs in the bottom of the ninth, Sam emerged from behind the fence silently repeating Tommy Lee's advice from earlier. She was scared she would foul up her turn but that inner monologue was interrupted by the overwhelming support coming from her teammates. "Come on Sam! You can do it!" they roared. Jonas laughed to himself, thinking what fools these boys were for not realizing Sam was a girl.

The bill of Sam's red cap nearly covered her eyes. She lifted the bat from the ground and settled into a stance, forgetting to take any practice swings. As the mob's negative energy suffocated the air around her, she remembered their wickedness. She remembered all the misery Jonas had caused her in the short amount of time since she and their mother had moved to Eugene. Sam pushed her cap bill out of the way, so she could see everything clearly. Before the first pitch was delivered Tommy Lee could sense the sudden transformation in Sam's mood. He wasn't sure what to make of it. Sam's first swing produced a slow roller between first and second base. The mob infielders charged the ball, but the throw to first was a split second behind Sam. "Safe!" the umpire announced, and at the same time Jimmy slid into third and Skip landed on second.

Now the pressure was on Billy but Jimmy had always said that pressure was Billy's middle name. He stepped up to the plate with the bases loaded, two outs and the game tied. He gave Sampson his dirtiest look. Billy then looked to Jimmy who had one foot on the third base bag and the other stretched toward home plate. Billy knew his responsibility to the team was to bring his brother home. Meanwhile, Tommy Lee was beside himself praying that Billy did not botch everything up.

The first pitch was a fastball and Billy tipped it into foul territory. This would surely be a depressing day for the boys if Billy didn't make something happen and quick. On the next pitch, another fastball, Billy had shortened his stance and moved up to the plate, looking for something slow. "Strike two."

After two fastballs, the next pitch was a change-up, the first one Billy had seen in the game. The mob had no clue this was Billy's favorite pitch. His sharp eye read the pitch like a hawk and he swung and connected with a loud crack that echoed across the field. The ball screamed into left field and Felix did everything he could to reach the ball. He scooped it up on the hop and made a desperation throw to Jonas at home plate.

The play would have never been close had Jimmy not slipped to the ground in his excitement to reach home plate from third, after seeing Billy's hit land safely in the outfield. Fortunately, Jimmy got back on his feet right away.

Jonas stood up and tore off his mask. He held forward his glove and positioned himself to block the plate. Felix's throw was high but Jonas was still bound and determined to somehow make the catch. Jimmy was coming at full speed and everyone's hearts were pounding. Jonas knew he would have to make a one—or two-foot leap into the air to make a successful catch. He reached his mitt high above his head and jumped. The ball smacked into the fingers of his mitt just as Jimmy dove straight into him. With a giant thud, the two enemies fell to the ground, one on top of the other. Jonas's hands flew back and the ball rolled down his arm and hit the dirt. Jimmy took quick notice of the loose ball and scrambled a step backward to tag the plate.

"Safe!" Coach Fleming bellowed, seemingly to the entire state of Mississippi. The good guys had won! The final score was 6-5. The baseball diamond was officially theirs. A fumbled baseball at home plate and their lives would never be the same again.

The joy that exploded from the stands sounded like a symphony of drums and trumpets as Hoorays blared from the fans of the winning team. The boys all gathered around home plate for a celebration and their fathers, uncles, brothers and friends quickly joined them. But in all the commotion, Sam silently slipped away. Her disappearance went unnoticed, as did the mob's blunt and bitter exit with their families trailing behind offering condolences. On their way out, Sampson made it a point to run into T.J.

Sampson's eyes were red with hate as he spoke just loud enough for only T.J. to hear. The words stung T.J. like a dull knife and left an ill feeling in his stomach. "I oughta get myself a white hood and come string your ass up on a tree tonight . . ."

"That's enough boy!" Sampson's father warned him and directed him away from T.J.

Unaware this had just happened, Tommy Lee slapped Billy and Jimmy with high fives and congratulated them all for their hard work and talent.

Farmer Hayes came to the center of it all, holding up his mother's expensive new Kodak. He asked the boys to gather together for a group photograph. T.J. was nowhere to be seen. He knew, regardless of being on the winning team, he would not be welcome at Eugene's annual picnic.

Jimmy and Billy stood together in the center with everyone else around them. Just before Famer Hayes called for the boys to say "Cheese" Jimmy turned to Billy and said, "This ain't right. We need to find T.J."

"You're right," Billy agreed. "Wait! Farmer Hayes. Excuse me sir but," and then he and Jimmy turned and looked at all their friends, "we need to find T.J. y'all. He belongs in this photograph. He deserves it."

"I was just about to say the same thing," said Skip. "And Sam too, we need to find them both."

Everyone agreed. Now the dilemma was how to find them? Tommy Lee was within earshot and informed them of the direction T.J. was heading when he took off into the woods. As for Sam, Tommy Lee assured them that he was long gone by now and they had a better chance of catching up with T.J. The photo would just have to be taken without Sam. The boys did not waste any time and fortunately, as soon as they stepped into the woods, they spotted T.J. They called for him and he turned around. Skip ran to catch up with him. It took a bit of twisting of T.J.'s arm but a look of pride came over his face when he finally agreed to return for the photograph. The boys were so happy to have him included. They would have felt terrible, in years to come, if they had not stopped Farmer Hayes before he pulled that Kodak's lever and gone after T.J. It was now a captured moment for them to hold onto and keep forever. As soon as the photograph was taken, T.J. was gone again.

"Come on, friends! We've got ourselves a Fourth of July picnic to attend!" Pastor Cook announced with the usual gleam of hospitality in his voice.

The citizens of Eugene cheerfully made their way to Daisy's Pond. The remainder of the evening was brimming with traditional community festivities. All the wives had been busy that week preparing a mouthwatering summer feast for everyone's appetites. There was fried chicken, shrimp gumbo, chicken livers, butter beans, fried okra, turnip greens, black-eyed peas, collards, egg bread, cornbread, popovers, boiled peanuts, ambrosia, bread pudding, cobblers, pies, homemade ice cream, fresh-squeezed lemonade, sweet tea and, of course, plenty of sweet corn. The main course was a 250-pound hog, which had been slow-roasted over a smoldering pit since morning. Jimmy and Billy could not recall ever before seeing so much delicious-looking food at their fingertips. It was excruciatingly painful to be patient and wait for Ellen's permission before filling their plates.

Laughter-filled sack races, egg tosses, and a watermelon-eating contest entertained everyone. The sunshine streamed down and kept the thick, green grass warm beneath the feet of barefoot children who were running about, laughing and playing. Throughout it all, Sam still was nowhere to be seen. The boys asked around but no one had seen or even heard of a Sam aside from that day's game.

"That's so strange that Sam just disappeared," Billy mentioned to Jimmy.

"Yeah, and I feel guilty that T.J.'s not here either. It ain't right."

"I know. He deserves to be here just the same as anyone else," Billy agreed.

"Well, people are linin' up for food. You comin'?"

Jimmy shook his head no. "Not right now. I will in a bit."

After covering his arms and neck with a dose of calamine lotion, Jimmy went into the woods to look for T.J. He had a suspicion that T.J. had not gone all the way home and he was worried about him. It took Jimmy a while but finally, there, beneath a canopy of green, seated and hunched over on a tree stump, sat T.J. His utter gloom slowed Jimmy in his tracks.

"Hey," Jimmy said softly, just a few feet behind T.J.

T.J. was startled by Jimmy's voice and hastened to wipe his face dry. He wanted to say something, but waited to see if Jimmy was going to continue.

"I gotta give you a heap of credit, my friend, for even agreein' to be a part of that game." Jimmy's tone was whisper-like and sincere.

"I know you weren't yourself today but you played great. We all thought so." After this, Jimmy wasn't sure of what to say next.

"Why is there so much hate?" T.J. asked in a fragile voice.

Jimmy could hear T.J. speaking, but couldn't understand the words with T.J.'s head down and his hands covering his mouth. "Huh? I'm sorry. What did you say?" Jimmy felt bad for asking.

T.J.'s anger had been building up for so long that he knew if he continued to stifle it, it might eat at him forever. T.J. was not about to let this happen. So he stood up and spun around to face his friend.

"Ah said why is there so much hate? How's come you don't hate me? Ah'm a Negro and your not, so why's don't you hate me Jimmy McGee? You oughta. Ah mean, dat's just the way it's gotta be! It's how the world's always been."

Jimmy felt sad for his friend. "Yeah but T.J., that ain't the way it has to stay and you know it! It's wrong for them boys to be hatin' on you. It's wrong for anyone to hate. My daddy says bein' prejudice is a sad thing because God sees hate as a sin, so that makes it wrong. I'd bet if them mob boys weren't so ignorant to act the way they do they'd take to likin' you, just as much as we have. I say forget about the mob T.J. They ain't nothin' but trash."

"So dat gives then the excuse to go on doin' such things. You know, my daddy's always sayin' dat dis town is far betta than most in the South, 'specially 'round here. But does dat mean Ah ain't supposed to be tired of bein' afraid of goin' into a store or havin' to remember which side of da street Ah can walk on? And my mama says: Be lucky son! Dem boyz don't have to let you play. So be lucky they're willin' to. Jimmy, why should you and Ah's mixin', be referred to as luck? Just 'cause our skin looks different?"

Jimmy didn't have an answer and T.J. resignedly returned to his seat and buried his head in both hands. Jimmy walked around the log and sat down beside his friend, wrapping an arm around him. Just then, T.J. winced as he felt a hand on his injured shoulder. It was Skip's hand.

Skip yanked his hand away realizing T.J.'s shoulder was still tender. "Sorry."

T.J. turned around to acknowledge Skip. Skip offered his apologies for exposing T.J. to such a high risk.

"Ah wanted to play Skip," T.J. assured him. "None of dis is y'alls fault."

"I know, but . . ." Skip replied and then let out a long sigh. "I dunno. I'm just sorry T.J."

"So what's dis contract all about?"

Jimmy and Skip looked at one another with concern. Neither had prepared for this discussion. However, they knew it was best to approach it with full honesty even though it would hurt T.J.'s feelings. Skip proceeded to carefully explain their intentions and T.J. did his best to understand that the contract was made only with his best interest and safety in mind.

"Well, Ah best be gettin' home," T.J. said.

"I'll walk you," Skip offered. He was worried after the events of the day that one or more of the mob boys might be hiding in the woods waiting to pounce on T.J.

"We'll both walk you," said Jimmy.

"Ah'll be fine. There's still enough light. But thank you." T.J. looked both Skip and Jimmy in the eyes and earnestly smiled. "Thank you for everything."

In the near distance, the romantic wails of Farmer Hayes's fiddle could be heard. Night was gradually beginning to fall and the mosquitoes were on the hunt. In an hour or so, an orchestra of fireworks would light up the sky above Daisy's Pond. T.J. said goodbye and began his walk back to Slytown and Skip and Jimmy returned to the party. As they approached, they could hear Ellen scolding Billy amongst all the other chatter and laughter.

Apparently, Billy had convinced Jordan that the watermelon seeds he had eaten would grow into actual watermelons inside of him and eventually his stomach would stretch so far it would explode into a million pieces taking the rest of poor little Jordan with it. At first, Jordan hadn't believed a word of it, but Billy was too persuasive. He reminded Jordan that all a seed needs to grow is water, "and there's water in all that lemonade you been drinkin'.

Plus, every time Mama and Daddy make you drink water with supper, that seeds just gonna get bigger and bigger and bigger until BAM! . . . you're a thousand pieces layin' everywhere all over the dinin' room table!" It took nearly half an hour to calm down the two-year-old's sniffling.

Jimmy's eyes were wide with anticipation to hear from Billy what he had done to get their little brother so upset. When Billy told him, Jimmy burst into laughter. "You're a gas, Billy. And by the way, good game today!" Jimmy congratulated.

"You too twin! Where you been anyway?"

Jimmy explained that he went into the woods looking for T.J.

"You find him?"

Jimmy nodded and his stomach growled.

Billy asked if T.J. was all right and Jimmy just shrugged his shoulders and said, "I reckon."

"Well, if anything, at least, I reckon we won't have to worry about Jonas and his boys comin' around no more."

Just then, Skip and the others walked up.

"Thank the Lord for that!" said Philly. "I can't take no more of them damn boys."

"Phillip Tupper," warned Ellen, from nearby, with a stern but soft tone.

"Oh! Sorry ma'am." Philly didn't realize how loud he'd been.

Then, Ellen walked over. "Boys, I must say though," she said. "It was so nice of y'all to allow that new girl in town to join your team in Whitey's absence."

The boys all looked at one another with blank stares. "Girl?" they all thought to themselves. Then Billy realized to whom his mother was referring and instantly chuckled.

"Mama!" He chuckled again. "That wasn't no girl! That was our friend Sam!"

Philly, Boston and Fist began to laugh.

"I can't wait to tell Sam that your mama thought he was a girl," said Fist.

But Jimmy, Skip and Charlie weren't laughing. They looked at one another with suspicion and an uncomfortable knot began to form in their stomachs. Charlie gave Skip a look as if to suggest initiating this as an emergency topic of discussion. But Skip was quick to shut him down. He thought it best not to explore this possibility anytime soon.

12

~⚮~

In late August, overnight, both Jimmy and Billy sprouted pubic hair. Billy was overjoyed with relief but Jimmy felt quite uncomfortable with the new look.

"Waitaminute," Billy paused and said to Jimmy. "Do we gotta comb out the curls of all them hairs down there?"

Jimmy rolled his eyes. "No, you fat-head. But I'll tell you what—I'm definitely shavin' mine off," he decided.

"You can't do that!"

"I can do whatever I want. They're my pubes and they itch."

"Suit yourself. Just don't accidentally cut off your pecker."

Billy had also, finally, began experiencing wet dreams and a regular pattern of erections. He was so proud of himself. Jimmy, on the other hand, was still a "late bloomer."

"You know what? I think my balls got bigger!" Billy claimed.

"Shut up! They did not."

"No, I'm serious! I really think they did! Check yours!"

"Come on Billy, we best be gettin' to Grama and Grandpa's."

"Not before you check yours! Go ahead!"

Reluctantly, Jimmy did as instructed and was surprisingly satisfied to find that his brother's preposterous suggestion was accurate.

"Good call Billy!" Jimmy acknowledged.

"You know I've always had your back brother! Now I got your balls too!" Billy laughed.

Jimmy laughed back.

The entire walk to Grama and Grandpa Purdy's, Rose McGee kept a clear but close distance from her brothers. She was on a mission to see whether or not they'd follow their mother's instructions and pick up Grama's large roasting pan for Sunday's supper. Jimmy and Billy had a history of becoming distracted on errands and returning home empty-handed. Rose was banking on this happening today, so she could finally get some revenge after they refilled her shampoo bottle with raw eggs last Friday. Originally, Ellen assigned Rose to the trip, but Billy offered so he could swing by Bing's Toy Shop in town and check out the new Mustang B-47 model, for the umpteenth time. Jimmy tagged along just because.

The boys knew what Rose was up to and tried their best to out walk her but she was stubborn. Finally, Billy yelled over his shoulder. "Do you gotta follow us?"

Now that the twins were acknowledging her, Rose was prepared to state her point. "You know, in all honesty, I have good reason to believe that neither of you are capable of . . ."

"Nobody cares!" Jimmy cut her off.

"Excuse me?" Rose snapped.

"You heard him," said Billy. "Besides, why do you gotta be such an ol' fuddy-duddy anyway?"

Then suddenly, Rose felt an unidentified sharp object slice through the paper-thin sole of her left slipper and into her foot. First she screamed, loudly, then rolled back on her behind and tore off the shoe. Jimmy and Billy continued on, as if their ears heard nothing. Rose looked up at them and her brown eyes began to swell with tears. Jimmy turned around, expecting the problem to be trivial like a rodent blocking her path or something. He looked down at the road, but saw nothing except dirt and scattered stones.

But he stopped and squinted his eyes for a closer look while Billy urged him to ignore their sister and continue on.

Rose leaned forward and lifted her foot to see underneath. A trail of blood oozed everywhere fast and as she touched it, something cut into her finger. With this, the rest of her body collapsed to the ground. The boys looked at one another with panic and ran to their sister's rescue. They saw the blood and shuddered. When Billy yelled into Rose's ear for her to wake up, he got no response.

"Oh my gosh!" Billy panicked. "She ain't dead is she?"

Jimmy felt around for a pulse but wasn't really sure where he should be looking and felt awkward reaching for Rose's heartbeat. Then he realized she was breathing.

"Duh," he thought to himself.

"No. I reckon she just fainted."

Jimmy drew his handkerchief from his back pocket and tried soaking up some of the blood. With a clearer view, he could see a thick piece of glass protruding from the center of Rose's foot. He quickly took off his shirt and used one of its sleeves to wipe the injury clean for examination. The glass took almost no effort to remove and was as big as Jimmy's thumb. Jimmy balled up a handful of his shirt and applied direct pressure to the wound. It was clear that Rose needed to go home at once.

With not a car in sight, Jimmy and Billy realized they would have to carry Rose. She wasn't too heavy, so with the both of them working together, in a chair carry, they maintained a steady pace. But it became difficult once the road began to slope upwards and their grip began to slip. Jimmy suggested stopping to catch their breath but Billy was panicking and didn't want to waste anytime in getting Rose home.

"Wait," Jimmy stopped and slightly turned his head. "I hear something." He carefully set down Rose's legs, turned around and squinted his eyes to see through the distant waves of heat and dust. In the distance he saw a giant dust cloud and in the midst of it was a familiar-looking vehicle. "It's the sheriff! Hot dog! He'll help us."

They moved over to one side of the road and gently laid down their sister, who was still unconscious. Their backs were in knots. Jimmy ran into the middle of the road and waved his arms back and forth, as if flagging down a rescue plane.

Sheriff Buford T. Justice was essentially the town hero. For the past twenty-five years he had seen to it that folks could leave their doors unlocked at night. Eugene had a low crime rate to begin with, but whenever something suspicious arose and called for investigation, Sheriff Justice had demonstrated over and over that he was already on it.

He pulled up alongside the boys and inquired about Rose's condition. Because the boys were short of breath, they were momentarily speechless. He stepped out of his car and drew himself up to his full height. Jimmy showed him the piece of glass. The sheriff was a sturdy gentleman with silver hair, a dark handlebar mustache, and a husky voice. He inspected the piece of glass for any signs of jagged edges but the entire piece appeared flush. He then knelt down to examine Rose's foot for swelling or bruising around Jimmy's bandage. Although the sheriff did not appear too concerned, he hurried to lift Rose up and carry her over and into his vehicle.

"How long has she been unconscious?" he asked.

"A couple minutes, maybe five," said Jimmy.

"You boys are gonna have to sit up front. Now hustle up."

Jimmy and Billy's faces lit up and they rushed over.

Suddenly, Jimmy remembered the roasting pan still at Grama's. Sheriff Justice told them that as soon as Rose was safe at home, he would help the boys out with a lift.

Ellen was giving the Hoover its Friday once-around the living room rug when the police car pulled up into the driveway. Billy and Jimmy ran into the house calling for her. At first, she thought the boys were in some kind of trouble and they were trying to cover it up. But as soon as she saw Justice carrying in her limp daughter, Ellen panicked. Justice laid Rose down on the couch and Ellen nestled down beside her. The boys explained everything that they knew, which wasn't much since they had been ignoring Rose prior to and at the moment of the accident. Ellen thanked the boys and the sheriff for their efforts. She then told Billy to run upstairs to the bathroom and grab a pair of tweezers and the antiseptic and sent Jimmy to the kitchen for the cold compress. The boys returned within moments and just as Ellen was about to apply the antiseptic, a gentle breeze came through the front window and settled upon Rose's face. Her eyes popped open and she looked strangely about the room wondering why she was back at home. Suddenly, Rose felt something cold sting her left foot. She jolted up with wide eyes, nearly causing Ellen to spill the bottle.

"Lay back down honey, everything's okay," Ellen promised. "I'm almost done."

Rose turned her head and saw her brothers standing in the living room entryway. Her questioning expression turned downright curious when she saw Sheriff Justice standing with them. Suddenly, everything came back to her. She could feel the glass stabbing her foot and remembered all the blood. Ellen told her to take slow, deep breaths as beads of sweat began to form on Rose's forehead. Then, Ellen gently pressed the ice-cold compress against Rose's cut and asked Jimmy to fetch her the magnifying glass from the desk beside him. Just as Ellen went to examine the cut, fresh blood oozed from the wound and obstructed her view. Ellen wiped that away and moved in closer with the magnifier.

Ellen could see no more glass through the lens but, just to be sure, handed it to Sheriff Justice so he could have a look for himself. If any shards were left in the wound, in time they would enter her bloodstream. Justice also saw nothing, and so finally Ellen allowed herself to somewhat relax. That's when she noticed that her boys were not in possession of the roasting pan. She inquired as to its whereabouts and Sheriff Justice spoke up with his offer to give the boys a ride out to their grandparent's house to pick it up. Ellen instructed Jimmy to go upstairs and put on a clean shirt before they were free to leave with the sheriff. "And be quiet about it, I just put your brother down for a nap."

Ellen looked upon Rose with a tender matter-of-fact expression and inquired: "Rose sweetie, aren't you a little too old to still be nosin' around over your brother's business?"

"But Mama . . ." Rose wanted to explain the whole shampoo bottle shenanigan.

"No buts Rose," was all the more Ellen had to say about that. "Now lay back down. I want you to stay off that foot, at least, till your daddy gets home."

Ellen stood up and walked over to Sheriff Justice to shake his hand.

"Thank you so much for your help."

"Anytime ma'am."

Jimmy came downstairs and he and Billy stood beside their mother, eagerly waiting to leave with the sheriff.

"Well, my goodness. Ain't that amazing," he proclaimed. "Your boys are growin' up ma'am. They're almost as tall as you now."

Ellen was 5'6" and the twins were now just two inches shy of her. She smiled and nodded with a wistful sigh.

"Oh, believe me sir, we are well aware of this," Billy commented.

Both Jimmy and Billy were smiling.

Sheriff Justice couldn't help but laugh. "I reckon so boys."

The next morning, the boys were out of bed and dressed in a flash. They had taken care of their baths the night before by employing a trick that worked every time: stirring a pocket-full of dirt into the tub water, the murky water appeared as though they had actually gotten in. They both hated taking baths and so, once in a while, this was a clever way out, assuming they never got caught. It was almost ten o'clock, so they ran to the schoolyard, where Skip, Charlie, Philly, Boston and Fist had already assembled. Sam had previously declined the invite with the excuse of having to remain home to help his mom clean.

On the Saturday before the start of a new school year, it had always been their tradition to go swimming. The journey to the swimming hole involved a half-hour trek along a beaten-down path through the dense-wooded forest, which ended just before the swamplands began. There was much to gawk at as generations of folklore the boys had grown up hearing, spooked along the marshy ground that stretched out beneath the surrounding canopy of green. Their rowdy arrival upon the swimming hole did not disrupt the chorus of crooning birds that remained camouflaged among draperies of Spanish moss and willow branches that eerily swayed, like phantoms, over the wide-open pool of water. On the far side, a tire swung from a sturdy oak branch. It was picture-perfect.

The boys stripped down to their underclothes and dove into the cool water. Engaged in games like Marco Polo and shark attack, they forgot the rest of the world entirely that afternoon. And Jimmy and Billy both, put Rose's injury behind them as they partied away the afternoon. They were so wrapped up, in fact, that not one of them noticed that someone was watching this supposedly private spectacle.

The spectator was hiding behind the trunk of an oak tree, about 15 yards away. Though she heard the boys laughing and shouting, she could make out very few words. The 14-year-old voyeur's name was Sarah Armstrong. Her wistful blue-eyes were particularly fixed on Jimmy McGee and, in the day's heat, she pushed her damp autumn-brown bangs back to get a better view. Sarah had grown up surrounded by older, prank-playing, male cousins, so it was a wonder this graceful young lady wasn't more like a tomboy. Still, their mischievous behavior had influenced her with enough boldness to not be afraid to spy on boys.

As the sun marked the end of the afternoon, the boys stepped out of the water and began to gather up their clothes. Much to their dismay, it was time to return home.

"Hey fellas, y'all see my clothes anywhere?" Jimmy asked, looking around.

Some of the boys looked around and shrugged.

"I put them right here," Jimmy said, pointing at a tree stump.

"Well they couldn't have just walked off. You must have put them somewhere else and just forgot," said Skip.

"You better find them quick Jimmy, we gotta hurry home," Billy reminded him.

"I know, but I sure can't go nowhere half-naked, now can I?"

All the boys began scouring the area. Within a minute, Jimmy was standing in front of the tree where Sarah Armstrong was hiding. Her heart stopped as she held her breath. She was trapped. Jimmy McGee was just on the other side and there was no way to escape. But then again, Sarah was enjoying this. She clenched Jimmy's clothes tight against her chest and secured her back flush against the tree's trunk. The leaves on the ground were crunching from Jimmy's nearing footsteps. Sarah turned her head to see exactly where Jimmy was and as she did, the two were standing face to face.

Sarah tucked the clothes behind her back as Jimmy froze up solid. There, just inches away and slightly shorter than his half-naked self, was a member of the opposite sex. Their startled eyes locked and Sarah's became glazed over with pleasure as she feasted on Jimmy's good looks. Jimmy, on the other hand, was experiencing something quite different. First of all, he was surprised out of his wits. He recognized Sarah but wondered how in the world she got there. Secondly, there was a severely awkward throbbing sensation beginning to advance upward from his pelvic region. "What the heck is that?" Jimmy shuddered to think. Suddenly, he realized. "Oh my God," his thoughts gasped. And, yes, that was his swollen member that had just breached his boxer shorts and was now staring straight up at Sarah. Jimmy did not want to look down but he couldn't help it and what he saw, horrified him. "Oh my God!" he gasped to himself again.

As Sarah stood there observing Jimmy's reaction, she too looked down to see what had captured this boy's attention. Immediately, she choked up in shock. As Jimmy noticed that Sarah was struggling to stifle her laughter, he decided that right now would be as perfect time as any to die!

Sarah lifted her eyes and stared into Jimmy's. As she struggled between feelings of empathy and mirth, Sarah's whole face began to tremble. Of course, not laughing would have saved Jimmy from further humiliation, if that was even possible at this point, but Sarah was so taken by Jimmy's adorable virtue that she could hold back no longer and started giggling. "Nice," Jimmy thought, less than appreciative of this girl finding any humor in his moment of disgrace. Sarah quickly regained her composure and extended her hand.

"Hi, in case you don't know me, I'm Sarah," she stated. Jimmy didn't move. "I live over on Whipple Avenue, behind the Wilson plantation. You live next to Mrs. Hayes don't you?"

Jimmy could not understand why this girl was talking to him so matter of fact, given his circumstance. With no reply from Jimmy, Sarah continued on. "She's such a sweet old lady. I walked by last week when you and your brother were over chattin' with her on her porch. I believe it was Tuesday mornin'. I don't suppose you saw me though nor did I want to impose."

"Impose? That's an understatement," Jimmy thought to himself. The girl's voice sounded sweet and friendly, but Jimmy didn't care. "Where in the heck is my brother?" Right about now Jimmy was aching for some security. He could hear the voices of his friends but they sounded faint as if they were a mile away.

"I can't wait for school to start on Monday. Can you?"

Again: no reply.

This was followed by a moment of silence. Sarah had a million thoughts running through her mind and was trying to pick which direction to take next.

Meanwhile, Jimmy was thinking: "My clothes. Where are they?"

As if Sarah had read Jimmy's mind, she brought her hands from around her back and held up his shirt and trousers.

"I reckon these belong to you," she stated plainly but seemed in no rush to return them. "Anyway, as I was sayin'. I saw you and your brother come into church late that one time. Did y'all get punished for that? I remember your daddy lookin' mighty sore."

As with her previous questions, Sarah expected no answer so this time she didn't wait before continuing on. Her motive was to keep Jimmy's attention (and his clothes) so he couldn't run off. She had never before seen him up close and, considering the circumstances, knew this might be her only opportunity.

Soon, Sarah realized that nothing she was saying was registering with Jimmy and then she noticed his lips were trying to force themselves open. She stopped talking and waited. After a moment, he came out with it: "C-could I h-have my, my p-pants back . . . p-please." The air had cooled down some and a nice breeze was wafting through the trees and between Jimmy's legs as his persistent member was still proudly staring up at Sarah.

"Oh. Of course." she answered awkwardly. "I guess I reckon I best be gettin' home too. Um, you know they say it might rain tomorrow. I sure hope not, my folks and I was plannin' on goin' on a picnic down at the pond after church. It's kind of a family tradition on the last day of summer break."

Jimmy reached out his hand for his clothes but, instead of handing them over, Sarah clutched onto them tighter and asked if Jimmy would be interested in joining her family on the picnic. Jimmy shook his head no and grabbed his clothes from Sarah and used them all to cover his lower half.

Sarah looked away and Jimmy struggled to get into his pants before he hurried over to his friends. He did not look back to see if Sarah was still standing there at the tree. He didn't care. He was humiliated and scarred by the entire experience as well as her boldness.

"Where have you been?" Billy wanted to know.

"Hey you found your clothes!" Fist noticed. "Took ya long enough."

"Looks like you found something else too," Skip laughed, looking down at Jimmy's crotch. "Congratulations buddy! That your first one?" Skip chuckled.

Jimmy looked down at his bulge and immediately adjusted himself. Billy's jaw dropped and Jimmy felt hot and dizzy. All he wanted to do was go home.

"So that's what you was doin' behind that tree all that time," Charlie joked.

Everyone, but Jimmy, had a laugh. All he could do was grab his brother by the arm and hurry off.

It wasn't long before Billy's arm grew sore from Jimmy's grip. He broke free and asked for the third time: "What's the problem Jimmy? Ain't you proud?"

Silence.

"Wait! Did something else happen back there?" Billy determined.

Jimmy wasn't certain whether or not he was ready to reveal the truth. He needed more time to sift through his beehive of thoughts. But the sustained silence worried Billy all the more.

When they arrived home 'Papa Won't You Dance With Me' was playing on the Philco radio. Billy could smell sweet potato soufflé and couldn't wait to devour a plateful. Jimmy didn't even notice. He just kicked off his shoes and rushed up the stairs.

"Jimmy? What about supper?" Billy asked.

"I'll be back. Just give me a minute. Alright?"

Billy watched his brother until he was out of sight before heading towards the kitchen. Ellen and Rose were about to set the table, and immediately called on Billy for some assistance.

"There isn't any mud on the bottom of your shoes, is there?" Ellen asked as she handed over the silverware to Billy.

"No, ma'am."

"Aren't you gonna ask me how my foot's doin'?" Rose demanded with her nose in the air.

"No," replied Billy bluntly.

"Mama?" whined Rose.

Ellen placed Jordan's booster seat on the chair beside hers. "You washed up yet Billy?"

"Yes ma'am," he lied.

"Get your brother. Supper's ready," Ellen lifted Jordan into his booster seat and pushed it up to the edge of the table. "Dear, it's time to eat," she called to Tom.

Wearing a blank stare, Jimmy came to the table. Throughout the entire meal, he never once looked up from his plate, even to laugh at Billy's reaction to Jordan's repulsive table manners. Hoping for some insight into Jimmy's distant mood, Tom asked the boys how their day went. But their answers were too shallow to derive any conclusions. Then, Tom tried to make small talk: "I heard from Pastor Cook a new family moved into town just this week. They got a son named Stuart. Jimmy, Billy, he'll be in y'alls class this year."

Billy looked over at Jimmy to gauge what his thoughts were on this news.

"Mama, Daddy, may I please be excused? I ain't hungry," Jimmy admitted.

"It isn't, ain't, it's I'm not hungry." Rose corrected.

"What are you my English teacher?" Jimmy snapped.

"Rose, leave it alone dear." Ellen instructed.

"But Mama?"

"Rose." Ellen did not want to hear another word of it.

Ellen honed in on Jimmy. His soufflé had received little attention and he'd taken but one bite from the roll. She wanted Jimmy to eat more, but Tom stepped in and excused Jimmy from the table. Jimmy stood up from the table and walked over to the front door.

"Where you goin' honey?" Ellen asked with concern.

"Um, would it be alright if I went on over to Tommy Lee's for a bit?"

"What for?" Ellen asked. "They're probably in the middle of supper right now."

"No, they usually eat around five."

"How long you gonna be?" Tom asked.

"Not too long. Maybe an hour."

"Well, all right. But come straight home after. You're gonna need a bath before church tomorrow," Tom approved.

Jimmy nodded and continued out the front door. Billy wanted to follow, but knew that whatever was going on with his brother, he would eventually be told.

As soon as Jimmy left, Tom and Ellen hounded Billy with questions. He swore he knew nothing. He only said that Jimmy almost lost his clothes and then, all of a sudden, he was in a real rush to get home.

"Perhaps he's feverish," Ellen suggested, now wishing she had made him stay home.

Finally, at eight-thirty, the front screen door creaked opened. Tom and Ellen were relaxing in the living room and looked up as Jimmy entered. His voice was low as he bid his parents goodnight. A new episode of Flash Gordon was on the radio but Jimmy appeared not to care. He continued up to the second floor and took his bath.

When the grandfather clock struck nine o'clock, Billy heard the attic bedroom door squeak open. Jimmy's footsteps followed! Billy sat up in bed with anticipation. When Jimmy arrived at the top of the stairs, he was still not his old cheerful self.

"How you doin?" Billy asked cautiously

"Tired."

"You goin' to bed now?" Billy did not want to go to sleep. He wanted to talk.

"Yeah."

"You sick?"

"No, just tired."

"Well, I don't wanna go to sleep yet. I wanna talk."

"Well, then go downstairs and talk to someone else. I'm goin' to bed."

Billy let out an exasperated huff and said: "Fine. I guess I'll just go to sleep too."

Jimmy got into his bed and closed his eyes. The lights now out, Billy lay with his eyes open, ignoring the choir of crickets outside and contemplating whether or not to say something. He knew Jimmy would only talk when he was good and ready. But Billy could not wait until then. His toes anxiously fidgeted beneath the sheets of his bed and after a while his brother finally spoke:

"Remember how I couldn't find my clothes this afternoon?"

"Yeah."

"Well," Jimmy began. "I couldn't find 'em on account of somebody else had taken 'em." Jimmy paused for a moment. "It was a girl."

Billy gasped.

"I think I've seen her around before, but I ain't too sure. Anyhow, she's the reason why I couldn't find my clothes."

"A girl? But, we were the only ones there?"

"That's what I thought too, but we weren't. You know the Wilsons?"

"Yeah, don't they got a little boy about Jordan's age? I know them. Why?"

"Well, she said she lives behind them, or somewhere close by. I don't really remember what she said."

"Behind 'em?" Billy wondered. "Oh, you mean Mr. Armstrong, the mayor?"

"Is that where the Armstrong's live? I thought they lived over yonder on Clemmet Avenue."

"They use to. But now they're in that huge house by the Wilsons. I thought you knew that. Her name's Sarah."

"Sarah, who's Sarah?"

"Armstrong's oldest," said Billy. "She's the mayor's daughter, Jimmy. I'm sure you've met her before."

"Maybe. I mean I recognized her and I'm sure she told me her name, but I don't know."

"Yeah," Billy understood. "So why'd she have your clothes?"

"How old is she?" Jimmy asked, trying to avoid Billy's question.

"Our age," Billy answered. "No wait, she's older. I think she's fourteen. Yeah, I remember hearin' somewhere that her daddy held her back a year in school. Otherwise, she'd be in Skip's grade, instead of ours." Billy paused for a moment. He was confused as to why Jimmy was so confused about Sarah and why she was suddenly on his mind. "You know she's in our class, right?"

Jimmy didn't answer. His face was turning red.

Billy then asked, "Jimmy, what happened to you this afternoon?"

Jimmy dragged out a sigh of frustration. "This cannot be happening to me."

Billy was becoming annoyed that Jimmy was ignoring his questions. But then, the missing piece suddenly popped into his head. "Waitaminute," Billy's voice trembled. "If she had all your clothes then you must've been standin' there . . ."

"Uh-huh."

"Oh geez! Are you all right?" Now everything had become serious and Billy sat up in bed. "Holy cow! She didn't see anything, did she?"

Jimmy drew in a deep breath and pulled his sheet up tight around his neck for security. In a long and turbulent second, Jimmy relived the entire episode and answered: "Yeah."

Billy's jaw dropped wide open and in a loud whisper he said, "Holy Mackerel! It's our first hard-on Jimmy!"

Jimmy was so annoyed by Billy's enthusiasm.

"I was so embarrassed, not only did it get real big, it stood straight up and came right outa my shorts and stared right up at her!"

"Did she stare back?" Billy was shocked and wanted to know more.

"The whole time," replied Jimmy.

"Oh my gosh," was Billy's initial reaction, but then, he began pumping his fist into the air and roared, "Heck yeah! That is the best story I have ever heard!"

"No it's not Billy!" Jimmy rejected.

Right away, Billy calmed down understanding his brother needed total empathy and not to be joked about.

A chill suddenly ran down Jimmy's entire spine and he pulled the covers up even tighter around his neck. He mumbled his first few words and Billy couldn't make them out. Rather than interrupting, Billy patiently sat there and listened. When Jimmy finally paused for a moment, Billy said: "So that's why you had to go to Tommy Lee's tonight. You just needed some advice." Billy tried to search for some comforting words but nothing came to mind. He then remembered that The Armstrong's attended their church. "Uh, Jimmy." Billy figured he might as well inform his brother now.

"I know," Jimmy read Billy's mind. "And there ain't no way on earth I'm goin' to church tomorrow. Plus, she's probably done already told all her friends. This is gonna turn into some huge scandal-like, I just know it."

"And that's exactly why I can't stand girls. They start too much gossip," Billy stated. "But how you gonna convince Mama and Daddy to let you stay home?"

Jimmy turned in his bed and looked over at the east window. The leaves of the oak tree right outside were shimmering from the moonlight. He thought to himself for a moment and then said, "I'll just have to play sick."

"And what about school on Monday?" Billy added.

Jimmy sighed. "I dunno. But I'll have to think of something."

About the Author

When I was just a young boy
I played under the table
Sun beat down upon my face
And stars dried my tears

Now that I'm older
The hills have become mountains
They've grown so tall I don't think I can see.

Oh I feel the wake of my sandbox empire sleeping 'neath the waves.
Oh inside my freedom waits for high tide to step outside these
imaginary walls.

Remembering the woodpiles
Dreaming they're a fortress
All my little toy soldiers marching to a beat.

Now those walls have reached so high
With Senators and taxmen
Perched on top… better hold on tight those walls are coming down.

And I feel like I'm suffocating in the forest
Lead me to some room

B.W. Gibson

Arm in arm we are marching on
to Freedomland we will head this army of love
Let your heart hear the beat of everyone
As they unite and step in time in harmony as one.

And as the night grows darker
I hear the army singing
To every new home I moved their music led the way
and through the trees of critics
and waves of so-called leaders
We're pounding doors and banging walls with every song we sing.